Fear rippled through her.

Her attacker was still at large somewhere, but Ruby did not think he would brave the sanctuary property, and definitely not with the police on the lookout.

Anxiety lingered in her veins, but she forced herself into action anyway. Her whole life had been steeped in fear that shadowed her every moment since her friend's disappearance, and she was sick of it. Finally, there was a chance to shed some light on that darkness, and she would not let the precious moment pass.

She had almost reached the tree when she heard footsteps running through the underbrush, moving fast, coming close. She slipped behind a screen of bushes, heart thudding. Her two brushes with death replayed in her mind. She felt the knife slicing into her flesh and felt the hot breath against her throat. The thoughts ratcheted her pulse even faster.

Stay hidden, she told herself. *You're safe.*

Not in these woods, her mind taunted.

Not anywhere.

Books by Dana Mentink

Love Inspired Suspense

DANA MENTINK

is an award-winning author of Christian fiction. Her novel *Betrayal in the Badlands* won a 2010 RT Reviewers' Choice Award, and she was pleased to win the 2013 Carol Award for *Lost Legacy*. She has authored more than a dozen Love Inspired Suspense novels. Dana loves feedback from her readers. Contact her via her website at www.danamentink.com.

HAZARDOUS HOMECOMING

DANA MENTINK

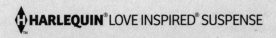

HARLEQUIN® LOVE INSPIRED® SUSPENSE

Recycling programs
for this product may
not exist in your area.

 LOVE INSPIRED BOOKS

ISBN-13: 978-0-373-67642-2

Hazardous Homecoming

Copyright © 2014 by Dana Mentink

Are not two sparrows sold for a penny?
Yet not one of them will fall to the ground outside
your Father's care. And even the very hairs of
your head are all numbered. So don't be afraid;
you are worth more than many sparrows.
—*Matthew* 10:29–31

To my two little birds poised at the edge of the nest.

ONE

Something glittered, garish and out of place against the massive framework of sticks that comprised the abandoned eagle's nest, a flash of metal, gold. Ruby Hudson shaded her eyes and peered through her binoculars at the aerie tucked high in the pine tree and moved to find out what the glittering object was. She estimated the structure to be a good two tons worth of tangled branches, no doubt added on to and reused by many generations of eagle pairs since her father purchased the land in the wilds of Oregon decades ago. It had been hemmed in by a tight clench of fir trees, recently removed due to borer beetle damage. The disease had taken hold throughout the area. Ruby had been distraught to watch the nearby trees cut down. So had Josephine Walker, who lived nearby.

"You can't cut them," Josephine had wailed. "My Alice won't be able to find her way home."

Alice won't be coming home, Ruby's heart had answered. Not after twenty years.

Now the sharp scent of the felled trees mingled with a small pain wriggling through her stomach again. If her family had never come, she wondered for the millionth time, would the tragedy have still occurred?

Stop it, Ruby. It isn't healthy. She loved the property, the birds, the endless blue sky and the smell of life burgeoning all around her. The Hudson Raptor Sanctuary had saved countless birds, it was a haven…and also the place where she'd first learned what evil was. The memory of Alice Walker came to mind, hair so fine it blew in the breeze like downy feathers, and eyes of… Had they been blue? It bothered her that she could not remember.

If the Hudson family—Ruby, her father and brother— had only remained in San Francisco it never would have happened, the one fleeting moment that changed them all forever. She slapped away a leaf that had become tangled in her auburn hair. Blue or green? She should know the color of Alice's eyes.

Her skin prickled as the leaves rattled out a hollow rasping chorus in the breeze. It had been a June day then, too. Ruby, desperate to play outside, had badgered her father until he acquiesced with strict orders—she was only to walk to the end of the graveled path and back with little Alice who had come to play.

No straying, Ruby.

The woods were dark and dangerous.

More than dangerous, she'd learned.

Deadly.

The hair on the back of her neck stood up, along with the feeling that there were eyes on her that very moment. The same sensation she'd gotten the day before, and on and off for weeks since the tree removal had begun. She suspected it was Josephine again, following her, begging her not to cut the trees that somehow preserved the hope that her daughter would return.

She listened. Nothing. There is no evil in these woods, she told herself firmly.

Then what happened to Alice all those years ago? She'd seen Peter Stokes that day, a jovial fifteen-year-old who lived nearby with his mother and little brother, Cooper. Peter had become the main suspect for a while.

He'd returned to the tiny town of Silver Peak four months ago, living in the rickety cabin just beyond the edge of sanctuary property. She wondered how she would feel if they came face-to-face. Was he a man she'd falsely accused? Or the person who hid the guilty truth from them all?

Ruby shook the clinging past aside and climbed up the rough limbs.

A drop of moisture fell from above and left a cold trail along her temple. She shimmied up, using the latticework of branches. She'd measured the nest before, adding to her study notes, a good nine feet in diameter, conical, wedged into the fork of the pine. The nest had been abandoned years before as the trees around grew taller. Eagles liked to have a clear, unobstructed view. The glimmer of gold was a few feet away and she had to take a precarious step out onto a lower branch to reach it. It creaked ominously under her feet. With straining fingers she stretched farther, past the bleached white bones of a rabbit and the glistening ribs of a long-dead trout. A few inches more.

Sweat beaded her brow in spite of the cool. She could not reach it, not without stepping out onto a weaker branch that would deliver her fifteen feet straight to the ground. She remembered the pencil behind her ear and used it to hook the gold object. It was stuck on a dried conifer branch, one of many wedged into the aerie by the male during incubation for some reason known only to eagles. She dislodged it, sending a cascade of brittle bones to the forest floor.

She scooted toward the trunk and stared at the object in her hands.

A necklace, small and delicate. Her heart froze over, the beats crystallizing in horror as she contemplated the heart charm hanging from the chain with a letter inscribed on it. A tiny *A*.

For Alice.

The child who had vanished without a trace that

long ago day in the dark and dangerous woods. It was as if all her memories flooded her mind in one horrifying rush. *Alice, Alice,* her mind cried out. What happened to you? Did Peter hurt you? Was it a stranger? What should I have done? The cold metal locket seemed to chill her palm.

Somehow, her body guided her down from the tree until she dropped heavily onto the soft cushion of needles.

She stared at the necklace dangling from her nerveless fingers.

"My baby's," came a sibilant whisper that made Ruby cry out.

She whirled to see a gaunt woman, gray eyes in a dead white face. Long silvered hair streamed over her shoulders. Her mouth was twisted in a horrified line. "That necklace. It belongs to my baby. I want it."

Ruby forced her mouth to work. "Mrs. Walker?" Ruby felt the hunger in Josephine's eyes, a ferocious need to connect to Ruby because Ruby was there and her daughter was not.

"It's Alice's. You took it. You took her. I see the truth now. It wasn't a stranger. Or Peter. It was you."

"No," Ruby started to say until anguish closed up her throat. She fought for breath. "Mrs. Walker, I don't know what happened to Alice. I did not see the person who took her. Remember? I told you before."

She pointed a finger at Ruby, the nail broken and dirty. "You wanted her necklace. Give it to me."

Fear arced violently inside Ruby. "I found it in the nest, up there."

Mrs. Walker did not look up. Her red-rimmed gaze never left Ruby's face.

"You took her."

"No, I did not. Alice was my friend. I would never…" Ruby's throat thickened as she fought tears. She moved back a step. "This is evidence. We can go to the police again. It might help them find her." She felt cruel saying it. After two decades they would not find Alice, not alive anyway. Everyone knew this, yet a tiny flame of hope never died inside Ruby, and she knew that flame must be a roaring fire inside the mother whose daughter had vanished without a trace.

Mrs. Walker cocked her head and for a moment, Ruby thought she understood. Then her eyes narrowed, mouth twisted. "I've been watching you. All these months, I've been watching you make your plans to hide your guilt. Did you think cutting down the forest would keep you safe?"

Cold rippled through Ruby's body. She could not reply.

"You took my daughter, and you want to take her necklace now. That was from her father. You cut down the trees so she can't find her way home."

"Mrs. Walker," Ruby whispered. "Please listen to me."

Mrs. Walker pulled a knife from her pocket. She gripped the white handle, the blade winking in the dappled light. Ruby's mouth went dry.

"You took my Alice."

Ruby could only shake her head, the necklace vibrating in her trembling hand.

"You took my baby," Mrs. Walker said again. With each word her voice rose in volume until it was a shriek that reverberated through the trees, startling two Meadowlarks into flight. "I want her back."

Ruby screamed and threw up her hand as the knife flashed toward her.

"Peter?"

No answer.

Cooper Stokes regarded the mess of a cabin his family had called home once upon a time. Though his brother, Peter, had returned some months before, dust blanketed the shelves, the carpet was dark with ugly stains and everything that had been worth a nickel had been hocked, no doubt. A mouse skittered along the top of the kitchen cupboard, regarding him with curious, twitching whiskers as if to ask why anyone of the human variety would choose to come here.

"No choice, mouse, so deal with it," he said, his voice odd and hollow in the silent space. It was a wreck, in much the same way his brother Peter's life had been for the past twenty years since suspicion cloaked him in a cloud of darkness from which he couldn't escape. Cooper sneezed, a wave of doubt rushing through him. He'd allowed himself to believe that Peter was sober, holding down a job, finally. Cooper's contract to work in the adjoining national forest seemed serendipitous. Go crash with Peter for a while. To enjoy the company of his sober brother? His darker thoughts took over. Or to check up on him?

It was incredible to think that Peter could again make a home here in this wreck, especially with the memories crawling around as numerous as the rodents.

Suddenly, he felt closed in by the space, though the high ceiling gave ample room even for his six-foot frame. Dust eddied around his feet as he escaped onto the front porch, sucking in deep breaths which calmed his nerves. The view outside made up for the disastrous interior. Pete's cabin backed onto the Hudson Raptor Sanctuary.

A sanctuary. Ironic. Peter had found no sanctuary there, not one friendly soul to believe in his innocence.

A scream split the air and he froze. Bird?

Another shrill cry. The hair on his arms raised as he determined it was not an animal sound, but human.

He vaulted over the split railing rather than taking time for the stairs and charged onto the sanctuary property, sprinting along a path in the direction from which he thought he'd detected the scream. Five minutes later he stopped, breathing hard. Trees crowded every square inch of the forest floor except for a narrow ribbon of trail that branched off into two directions. Which way? He listened.

Shouts now, instead of the scream, coming from the eastern fork of the trail. He barreled ahead, slapping branches out of his way. Small critters, maybe lizards, maybe not, scuttled away from his graceless progress.

Finally he emerged into a hollow, filled with cracked boulders that hemmed in a massive threesome of pines.

An older woman with long silver hair whirled to face him.

"What's wrong? Are you hurt?"

The woman didn't answer, but something in her eyes caused his pulse to tick up a notch. A vacancy in the pupils, insanity even.

Then he saw the knife in her hand, something dark staining the handle.

"She took my daughter," she said, voice low and soft.

"She?" Cooper dropped his gaze to the ground behind the lady, finally noticing what his brain did not want to believe. A young woman lay on her side unmoving, auburn hair covering her face.

"She needs help," he said, in what he hoped was a placating tone.

"No, no, no," the old woman chanted. "She took my girl."

The last word was gathered up by the wind that danced around the grove, caught along with the pine needles that drifted, lifeless to the ground.

He kept his voice low and level. "Whatever it is that you think she did, it's no reason to hurt her. Move away and let me help. Please."

The woman looked at the prone figure lying at her feet. "I had a girl once."

"So you know how sad her family will be if she doesn't come home."

She nodded, a sudden wash of tears coursing down her cheeks. "Yes." Her voice dropped to a whisper. "They'll be so sad because they'll never know."

He didn't follow, but there was no time to press the point. If the girl had been stabbed, she might be bleeding out. "Yes, very sad. Let me help her."

A long moment passed while the woman considered, hair rippling around her face. Abruptly, she shuffled into the trees, making her own way where there was no trail to be seen.

Cooper went to the victim, pushing aside the sheaf of hair. There was something familiar about the heart-shaped face, spattered with freckles, wide cheekbones and a delicate mouth. A bruise darkened her right temple.

She was breathing on her own. A blessing he'd take gratefully. He ran his hands along her slender arms and legs, checking both for breaks and blood. Everything appeared to be intact. Gently he lifted the bottom edge of her jacket, near a tear that pointed to the knife entry point.

There was a grunt from somewhere behind him, guttural and bearlike and Cooper felt himself being jerked back and slammed against a tree. He stared into the furious face of Mick Hudson. Things became clear in spite of the ringing in his head. The woman on the ground was Mick's sister Ruby, whom Cooper had not seen since she'd ruined his brother's life.

Cooper blocked an incoming punch and threw his own weight against the big man, knocking him back, but only for a moment.

"What did you do to my sister?" Mick barked.

"Nothing. I heard a scream. There was a crazy woman standing over her with a knife. She's hurt and while you stand here trying to take me down, she may be bleeding to death."

Mick considered for a split second before he knelt by his sister, shoulders still heaving. "Bee, honey?" he whispered in a tender voice totally out of keeping with his toughened face and fists. He looked from her to Cooper.

"You a doctor?"

"No, but I've got some medical training. I was checking for a stab wound when you jumped me."

Mick moved aside. "Well, help her then." He obviously did not remember Cooper Stokes, brother of the most despised man in the county. Just as well.

Cooper bent and resumed his examination. "Here," he said, pointing to a thin ribbon of blood bisecting Ruby's creamy skin at the waist. "She's cut, but it's not deep. She's got a bump on her head which might be a bigger issue. We should get her to a doctor."

"I'll do it. Thanks." Mick didn't wait for any more discussion. He lifted Ruby from the ground and plunged back down the path from which he'd come. Cooper flexed his shoulder, sore from getting shoved into the tree trunk. He should go back to the cabin, let go of the thought of the red-haired Ruby Hudson, especially after what she'd done. It was clear that if he dared to follow Mick there would be trouble.

Trouble?

That was just fine with Cooper. He'd had his share of it, and he wasn't going to shy away.

He took off through the dappled woods after Mick and his wounded sister.

TWO

Ruby registered two things—the cool wet towel being applied to her head and the worry creases on the forehead of her brother who was taping some sort of bandage to her side. She sat up with a hiss.

"Ouch. That hurts."

"You were stabbed. Not deep, just long," Mick said. "Taking you to the doctor anyway."

She shook the hair out of her face. "No, you're not. I'm fine, and we don't need to go to the doctor. We need the police."

"I didn't catch the lady," said a voice from the open front door. "Sorry, but your well-being seemed more important at the time."

Ruby blinked against the sunlight which rendered the speaker no more than a blurry silhouette. "Who…?"

"Cooper Stokes," said the tall man.

"Cooper? You're…"

"Peter's brother, yes. We haven't seen each other

in a long time. I think I was seven to your five when Alice was snatched, if memory serves."

Mick's eyes were cold steel. "You have no business here. Your mother called my sister a liar all those years ago when Alice disappeared."

"And your sister accused my brother of kidnapping. Peter's life was ruined and it seems to me that you all are doing just fine, so who has the bigger right to a grudge, I wonder?"

"Do you want him to leave?" said Mick to Ruby, "because I don't have a problem throwing him out."

"It would be harder than you think," Cooper said quietly.

Ruby was about to answer, but instead she cried out as Mick taped the bandage to her side. "Sorry, Bee." The tone was gentle until he turned back to Cooper.

"My sister's hurt. She needs to be left alone right now. No offense."

"None taken," Cooper said. "I'll be happy to go with you to the police if you need me. I'm what you call a witness, I think. I didn't see the attack, but maybe I can tell them about the lady with a bloody knife."

"The lady was Josephine Walker, and I'm not pressing charges." She heard Cooper suck in a breath. From the corner of her eye, his crew-cut blond hair glimmered in the light, and she could feel him tracking her every movement.

"That was Alice's mother?" Cooper shifted, eyes darting in thought.

"Of course you're pressing charges," Mick said. "Lady tried to kill you."

"She's not in her right mind. She's been following me for months, and she saw me find…"

Both men stood stock still.

She forced a businesslike tone. "I found Alice's locket. It was tangled in the branches of the abandoned eagle's nest."

Two sets of shocked eyes stared at her.

"Are you sure it belonged to Alice?" Cooper demanded, moving closer, hands on his waist. Stylish jeans, she noticed, well-cut shirt that molded to his trim body.

"I'm pretty sure, but she took it before she stabbed me. We need to talk to the police and get it back. It could prove…" What? Who had taken Alice? Where she had wound up? Or nothing at all.

Cooper's lips thinned into a tight line. "Maybe there's DNA on it that will prove finally that my brother was not the kidnapper."

"Your brother was never even charged," Mick said.

"Didn't have to be. He was a fifteen-year-old kid. The accusation, the looks, the way he was shut out, turned him into an alcoholic." Ruby looked at the floor.

"It wasn't an accusation. Your brother was in the woods that day. I saw him. It was a fact."

"He denies it, and he didn't kidnap that girl, but not one person in this town believed him, especially the two of you. The police questioned you also, Mick, didn't they? But people believed your story."

"Because mine wasn't a story, it was true." Mick shook his head. "I had a fight with Alice's father the night before. I left in a huff. End of story. If Peter was innocent, then he got a bum rap, but turning to alcohol was his choice."

"Maybe you should try being convicted by everyone who used to call you friend and see how you deal with it," Cooper snarled.

He was face-to-face with Mick, and both looked as though they could easily throw a punch.

"Enough," Ruby said. She stood so quickly her head spun and both Mick and Cooper put steadying hands under her arms, which she shook away.

"Sit down, Bee," Mick said. "Please."

"No. We have to go to town to talk to Sheriff Pickford so he can get the necklace from Josephine. It may finally be the clue that tells us what happened to her." Ruby was irritated to find that her eyes were wet. After so many years of fear, sorrow and a crushing weight of guilt, the answer might be at their fingertips, the answer to the question that had tortured her for two decades.

Alice, where are you?

She would not waste a moment. "I'm going," she said, reaching for her purse.

"I'll drive you," Mick said, in a tone that indicated he was dealing with a creature he could never hope to understand.

"All right then." In spite of the throbbing in her temples, she moved in as dignified a fashion as she could past Cooper to the door. Was it really a wall of anger that seemed to roil out of him like storm clouds, or was it her imagination?

"Thank you," she managed. "For helping me in the woods."

He gave her a courtly bow. "Anything for a damsel in distress."

Even a damsel you believe destroyed your brother?

Mick grabbed his cell phone. "I'll call dad on the way."

"Your father's still a private eye?" Cooper asked, arms folded as he slouched against the doorframe.

"Retired," Mick said with no further explanation.

Ruby thought it might be an opening to restore a more civil relationship between them. Whatever he thought of her, Cooper had gone out of his way to help. "Your brother…is he…okay now? I know he's living in the cabin."

"Sober, at the moment, and he's got a small job of some kind. Always wanted to be a firefighter, but they don't welcome people with his history into that line of work."

Ruby felt her stomach tighten. "I'm sorry."

"Me, too," he said, watching as Mick led Ruby out the door and to the car.

Cooper would not reveal it for a king's treasure, but he was reeling inside from the shock as he drove his pickup into town, sick with fear that the Alice Walker incident was abruptly springing back to life. He'd come back to make sure Peter had a home again, that he'd permanently given up living in a car or on the streets. What strange twist of circumstance was it that the whole sordid past should be ripped open now, like a poorly healed wound?

God, I thought you were on this? That the past was finished and done with? He and Peter had worked so hard to let go of what lay behind them and press toward the future. Wasn't that what it said in Philippians 3? He felt the old familiar stir of anger, the one he'd fought all his life to crush. He'd decided to read those words, in the tattered Bible left by his father before he'd died in a wreck before Alice was taken. Years later as a twenty year old, he'd eventually listened to a friend and mentor who had encouraged him into a small group where he fit in like a snowman in the Sahara. Slowly, slowly, the peace and comfort in that old book was seeping into his soul, but sometimes there were moments when it seemed too hard to hold on to in a world where there was seemingly no justice or peace.

He arrived at the sheriff's office a minute after Ruby and her brother did. They sat in a depressing wood-paneled room that had not changed since the fifties when Cooper guessed it had first been constructed. Sheriff Wallace Pickford was a big man with strong shoulders and the weathered skin of a person who spent time outside and liked it.

Pickford turned on an iPad that looked ridiculously small under his massive paws. Nonetheless, he opened a file with amazing speed considering he was only using his pointer fingers to type.

Pickford fixed a heavy stare at Ruby. "Mick says you're stubbornly refusing to go to the hospital. Do I have that right?"

Ruby's cheeks pinked, her coloring like a china doll Cooper's grandmother used to own. "We have to get the locket from Josephine. It might tell us what happened to Alice."

Pickford's eyes drifted to Cooper. "Hello, Mr. Stokes. You're back. Joining your brother?"

"Temporarily," Cooper said.

"Hmm. Bad time for both you boys to be back in town," Pickford said, fingers poised above the keys.

"Why shouldn't we be here?" Cooper said. "It's our property, and Peter hasn't done anything. He's got a right to live here and so do I."

Pickford shrugged. "Just thinking the climate

might not be good, since the Alice Walker case just officially reopened."

Cooper was about to tell the sheriff exactly what he thought of the climate, when a silver-haired, mustached man entered. Perry Hudson. Ruby's father was probably nearing sixty, if Cooper remembered correctly, but his shoulders were still square and his body trim and athletic.

Pickford's mouth tightened.

"Mick told me over the phone," Perry said, rushing to Ruby and assuring himself that she was unharmed. He raised an eyebrow at Cooper. "I think I owe you a thank-you for helping my daughter."

Cooper allowed his hand to be shaken. "Surprised you started with a thank-you."

Perry frowned. "I know we've got bad blood between us…"

"Because you tried to prove my brother kidnapped Alice Walker." Ruby flinched at his tone, but he didn't let it slow him. No more kid gloves. If Peter was going to claim any chance at a future, it was up to Cooper to lay the groundwork. Cooper's "live and let live" philosophy would not serve here.

"I investigated your brother," Perry said calmly, "because he was the likeliest suspect and he was in the proximity at the time."

"Which doesn't make him guilty. And your son Mick was close in age to Peter and in the same proximity."

Mick glared and started to answer, but Pickford cut him off.

"That's why we checked him out, too, as well as investigating Lester Walker," Pickford said. "Can we get on with the matter at hand? My wife has a pot of chili on the stove." He flicked a glance at Perry. "You know how good Molly's chili is, don't you Perry?"

Perry stared at him. "Yes."

Cooper didn't understand the subtext of whatever was going on between Pickford and Ruby's father. Hostility? Distrust?

Ruby detailed the encounter with Josephine Walker. "So we have to get that locket."

"All right," Pickford said, grabbing his radio. "Let's just go do that."

They did not make it farther than the front counter before the door banged open. Josephine clumped in, a shocked silence burying them all for a moment at her wild-eyed stare, her dress bunched and knotted, dirty hem dragging on the floor.

Pickford recovered first. "Mrs. Walker. Come into my office. We were just making plans to go see you." They returned to the back and he continued. "Ruby said you've got a locket. I'll need to have a look at that."

"He's coming back," she said. "He called me a few minutes ago to tell me so."

"Who has, ma'am?"

"My husband."

Cooper tried not to look disbelieving, but he knew Lester Walker had taken to acting strangely, convinced that the Hudsons or Peter knew something they weren't telling about his daughter's abduction. Days after Alice's abduction, he'd disappeared, too, though the police had no evidence to suggest he'd done anything to his daughter and had not even been in the county when she was snatched. Indeed the man was grief stricken, according to accounts that Cooper had heard. Lester hadn't been seen since, that Cooper was aware of.

Pickford fiddled with the three-hole punch on his desk. "Your husband is coming back, ma'am? Mr. Walker?"

She nodded, a smile of satisfaction pulling at her thin lips. "Yes, and he'll make sure my baby is found." Her eyes slid to Ruby. "You're going to pay now. For what you did."

"She did nothing," Mr. Hudson said.

"Oh, yes," Mrs. Walker singsonged. "Oh, yes."

Cooper saw delicate patches of color deepen on Ruby's cheeks.

"I did not hurt Alice, Mrs. Walker. She was my friend, and I've grieved every day since she disappeared." Her voice hitched, and she cleared her throat. "You need to give Sheriff Pickford the locket so he can have it DNA tested."

She glared at Ruby. "It's at home. My husband is on his way to get it. He told me when he called."

The chief held up his hands to soothe her. "All right. We'll just call your husband to talk it over. Okay? What's the number?"

"He doesn't have a cell phone. He called from a pay phone on his way to our house. He must have felt deep in his soul what was happening with our Alice, and he called just at the time we needed him the most. I told him about the locket."

"We'll go talk to him in person, then, at your place."

"That's a good idea, before anything happens to the locket." Ruby strode to the door.

"Not to be rude at all, Ruby, but this is a police matter now. You're not to tag along." The sheriff shot a glance at Perry. "Or any of the clan."

Cooper knew he was included in the directive, as well. Stay away. Let the police handle it. The last time he'd trusted the police to handle things, his brother had been brought in for questioning, turned into the object of hatred by the whole town. He wasn't going to intrude on an investigation, but he was not going to be the mild-mannered bystander either.

Ruby's expression was a blend of anger, determination and exasperation. He was struck by the fact that as much as he did not have fond feelings for the Hudson family, he could not deny that it was hard to tear his eyes away from Ruby. Her hair was the kind of rusty red found in autumn leaves, skin creamy and porcelain, but she was certainly not fragile. Ruby was dainty and graceful, but he knew there was steel running along her spine.

"He's right. Let's take you to the doctor and see to your injury," Perry said.

Pickford focused again on Josephine. "You're very fortunate that Ruby wasn't injured badly and isn't pressing charges, but that doesn't mean I won't take action if I believe you're intending to hurt someone. I'm going to insist you go speak to one of the doctors at the hospital right now."

Josephine frowned.

"Let's have you all wait outside for just a minute," Pickford said. "I need to make a phone call."

Mick was already heading to the door, looking relieved that he'd been sprung from the tiny, crowded room.

Perry thanked the sheriff and nodded to Cooper before he exited, as well.

Considering the Hudsons were low on the list of his favorite families, he could not explain why he took a step toward Ruby when Josephine walked by. Maybe it was the memory of Josephine standing over her, triumphant. Or the feeling that something about Lester's well-timed phone call felt wrong, like the scream of a chain saw cutting through a silent forest morning.

Josephine surged close and Ruby backed into Cooper's steadying arms.

"Now you're going to get what's coming to you," Josephine said, her breath stirring the hair around Ruby's face, one side of her mouth drooping slightly. "You'll be punished, just like you should have been all those years ago for hiding the truth about what happened to my girl."

Ruby's cheeks flushed and went pale as milk. He tightened his sideways embrace. "Accusations can ruin people, Mrs. Walker."

She peered at him. "Peter and the Hudsons. Both of them worked together to ruin my life. Lester said it was a conspiracy all along. But no more. Now it's time to pay."

He was unsure how to respond as she moved by and passed out of sight into the lobby.

Ruby broke from his grasp. "My family had nothing to do with this," she said, turning blazing eyes on his.

He felt the flush of anger and pride. "And neither did mine. Feels rotten when someone thinks you're a liar, doesn't it?"

He expected an acid response to match his own bitterness. Instead he saw her falter as the barb struck home. For a moment, he wished he could retract the words. No one escaped unscathed from that long-ago moment. No one.

"I'm sorry," he said. "That was…"

A shout from the receptionist interrupted his apology. Ruby and Cooper charged through the reception room and out the front door to find Josephine lying on the steps, eyes half-closed, Perry kneeling beside her.

"She collapsed," Perry said.

The receptionist covered the phone with one hand. "I've got an ambulance en route."

Sheriff Pickford addressed the few passersby who had hastened to help while an officer tended to the fallen woman. "Ambulance is on its way. Let's just give the lady some privacy."

"Isn't that Josephine Walker?" The question came from a whip-thin woman dressed in jeans and a denim jacket. "I heard she found her daughter's locket in the woods."

Pickford's thick brows drew together. "News travels at Mach 2 around here. What of it, Ms. Bradford?"

She flashed a smile. "You can call me Heather, Sheriff."

"I make it a practice to keep away from a first-name basis with reporters."

"Freelance writer." Heather kept the smile.

"Whatever."

"So it's true that the locket was found? The one that belonged to the abducted girl?" she pressed.

The ambulance made the turn onto the main road, lights flashing. Cooper thought a look of relief washed over Pickford. "No information now. Priority now is getting emergency medical help to Ms. Walker. I'll need everyone to step back and let our medics do their jobs."

Cooper stayed at a distance. Mick and Perry bookended Ruby, standing like protective pillars on either side of her as Josephine was loaded into the ambulance. He wondered what was going through Ruby's mind.

Would the investigation stall until Josephine was released?

And in the meantime, the locket, the clue to finally clearing Peter's name, was hidden somewhere, unaccounted for.

Heather was edging her way toward the Hudson family.

Perry immediately steered Ruby to the car and bundled her inside, but before he closed himself in the driver's seat he cast one look at the approaching reporter and Cooper saw something that surprised him on the older man's face.

Fear.

THREE

Ruby's eyes burned as she tried to decipher her miniature writing in the tiny notebook. She should break down and get one of those fancy tablets or iPads for her notes, but the whole notion of trekking around the forest with a computer seemed ridiculous. So she sat in the closet-size office, a converted shed, truth be told, transcribing her notes and typing them into the ancient desktop computer. The space was cramped, to be sure, but the little shed was tucked in a stand of coniferous trees away from the main house, with a view of the soaring mountains behind and sheltered by massive boughs alive with birds and squirrels. The sounds of the forest night shift commenced in earnest as the sun sank behind the mountains, beginning with the *Myotis* bat that flickered past her window. There was no finer office anywhere on the planet, she was quite sure.

She forced her mind back to the job at hand. *Barn Owl pair 0907 and 0665 (Ted and Flossie) have chosen a nesting site in barn on northwest corner of the property.* Her fingers paused as she pictured the stunning birds with the heart-shaped feathers framing fiercely intelligent eyes. Pride swelled inside her. It was a huge victory. She could not resist the self-indulgence. Ted had only been released on the sanctuary property three months before, after treatment at the avian hospital for an eye injury resulting from a pellet gun. Ted survived, thrived, found himself a mate and now if all went well, a little fuzzy family would begin their journey in the musty barn. It was another step toward the sanctuary goal of rebuilding a thriving community of wild birds.

She sighed as she tapped in the information, wishing she had someone else to share it with who could appreciate the triumph. Her last "boyfriend," if he could be called that, stuck around just long enough to land himself a job with the fire service. *I'm just not a bird guy,* he'd explained. That was an understatement. He grew increasingly more bored with her daily hikes to every forgotten corner of the sanctuary. And he couldn't comprehend her sorrow when she discovered a dead red-tailed hawk that must have been shot by a trespasser. How could someone not grieve the sight of an elegant creature massacred in such a way? Feathers broken and bloodied, proud eyes dulled by death. *It's just a bird,* Tony had said.

Just a bird. But weren't the littlest lives supposed to be worthy in God's eyes?

Are not two sparrows sold for a penny? Yet not one of them will fall to the ground outside your Father's care.

But Alice had fallen, or been snatched, just a tiny bird with her whole life to live, and God had not so much as lifted a finger. Ruby remembered in vivid detail the day they'd gone out into the woods to play together. She'd been distracted by something, a feather caught in the root of the tree, and scurried to find it. When she turned to show Alice, she realized her playmate had vanished, as if she was a tiny sparrow snatched up by a raptor.

Just a bird.

Just a child from a poor family that never had a chance to fly.

And her abduction had stripped something away from Ruby, too—her innocence, her ability to trust. Truth was, she'd never really shared with Tony the deep river of emotions that trundled along inside her. And at the heart of it, she'd been the tiniest bit relieved when he'd left. She swallowed. Perhaps the abduction also obliterated her ability to love anyone but her family.

"So where were you, God?" she asked the cracked ceiling tiles, "when Alice was taken?"

She looked at the clock again. Ten hours had passed since their meeting with the sheriff, and it was now nearly nine. Almost sundown and no word on Josephine or the investigation.

Had Sheriff Pickford retrieved the locket? Her stomach tensed. Maybe, at long last, they would know what happened to Alice. And what would it mean for Cooper? Exoneration for his brother? Or perhaps it would be the final proof that Peter had indeed been guilty all those long years ago. She pictured Cooper, shoulders braced, mouth set in a firm, determined line. He would be forced to acknowledge the truth. It should thrill her, but she found it only made her stomach knot a little tighter.

Pine needles crunched outside. She froze. Why had she stayed so late in the office? She took her phone out of her pocket. A quick text, and Mick or her father would be there in a flash.

Ruby, you've got to stop depending on them to keep you safe. Still, she clutched the phone and crept to the front window. There were so many thick trunks available for hiding places, so many shadows offering dark pools of concealment. She eased aside the worn white fabric that served as a curtain.

Knuckles rapped on the door, and she leaped backward, heart in her throat.

"Ruby?"

With a gusty sigh, she put down the phone and opened the door for Cooper. "You scared me."

"Sorry." He shoved his hands into the pockets of

his jeans. "Got some info. I should have left it with your brother and dad at the main house but…"

"But you don't like them."

"And they don't like me, which is odd, because I'm a hugely likeable guy." He offered a grin that set off the sparkle in his eyes. "Your brother has a tendency to put me in a headlock when we share airspace."

"He's a little overprotective. Former marine, you know."

"Yeah. Reassuring to know he's highly trained in ways to kill me. Anyway, I had a call from Heather Bradford. She wanted to talk about Peter and what happened. An interview is what she was really after, I think."

A painful fluttering began in Ruby's stomach. "I see. I heard she's been working on a story. It's why she came to Silver Peak, I think. Josephine mentioned something a few weeks ago about Heather, but I thought she was rambling. I think Heather's been dredging it all up for a 'twentieth anniversary of the disappearance' type of story." It was all flooding in again, still every bit as fresh and raw, as if the decades in between did not matter in the least. "Did you talk to her?"

"No."

Ruby started. "You didn't? Why not?"

"Dunno." He looked away at a lark that flitted in the branches from one twig to the next. A slight smile curled his lips as he contemplated the little bird. "I guess…" He sighed. "I know this situation is hard on everyone involved. I don't want to do anything careless that will deepen wounds."

"Pretty mature," she said.

"Yeah, not so much. Still a work in progress. Ten years ago I would have unleashed some serious venom to anyone who would listen, but these days…" He shook his head. "I need to think and pray about it before I talk to her."

To think and pray about it. The setting sun darkened his hair and painted the strong planes of his face.

She realized he was staring at her, waiting, perhaps for a response. "That sounds good. Certainly it's the smart thing to do, to be cautious." The weight of his green-gold gaze made her breath quicken. Her phone rang, and she snatched it up, gesturing for Cooper to step inside the crowded space as she answered. "Hello?"

"Ruby, I wanted to let you know that Josephine has had a stroke of some kind. She'll be in the hospital awhile, and she's unresponsive at the moment," Pickford told her.

"Will you go find the necklace anyway?" The words tumbled out before she thought them through.

He paused. "I'm going to give it a day. If she isn't coherent tomorrow, I'll get a search warrant and take a look."

"Tomorrow?" Ruby groaned.

"She said her husband was coming back. We'll keep an eye out and if he arrives, he'll let us in to look, I'm sure, or hand it over himself."

"But Sheriff, this is so important and Lester wasn't, um, stable. He might have been involved, all those years ago."

"There was never one shred of evidence to make us believe Lester did anything to his daughter."

"But, if anything happens to that locket..."

His tone hardened into stone. "Don't tell me how to do my job, Ruby. I'm the man in charge here, not the Hudsons." He sighed. "She's been through a parent's worst nightmare, and I know it's damaged her and Lester. She lost more than anyone, and her wish is to wait for her husband. I'm going to honor that, at least for twenty-four hours. I hope you can live with it."

It was clear. Whether she could live with it or not, that was the way Sheriff Pickford was going to proceed. She thanked him and disconnected before filling Cooper in. He listened, rolled his wide shoulders and let out a sigh.

"I'm becoming a pro at waiting around. Peter's been off somewhere. I haven't even seen him." She caught the flash of worry in his eyes.

"How long will you stay in town?"

"I'm taking a week of vacation, but I'll be in

the area for a while. Doing some work for the national park."

"What kind of work?"

"Logging borer beetle damage. I'm a botanist with the Forest Service."

She giggled.

"Something funny about that?"

She pressed hand to her lips. "I just remember when you were a kid, you picked all kinds of wildflowers even when I ordered you not to."

He grinned. "I gave you one, didn't I? When I asked you out on a date."

"Yes, but I refused to be placated by your paltry blossom."

"The rest were for my mom."

"How is your mother?"

"Lives at her sister's place in New Mexico. Peter stayed with her for a while over the years when he flirted with sobriety. Together we managed to pay for two stints in rehab." His voice grew soft. "It's not easy for her to see him like that."

Ruby felt shamed that she had never taken the time to wonder what had become of Mrs. Stokes after she moved away with Peter and Cooper following Alice's disappearance. They were the polite neighbors, a single mother with two boys who would wander onto the sanctuary property and explore it every chance they got. Ruby's father had never shooed them away and sometimes he'd even paid Peter to help out with some brush clearing. She suspected that he understood how hard it was to be a single parent, since he'd walked the same road after he lost his own wife to ovarian cancer when Ruby was a baby.

"Well," he said, turning to go. "I'd better get back in case my errant brother shows up. May I walk you back to your house?"

She hesitated only a moment. "Yes, thank you."

He stepped out on the porch and inhaled deeply. "This is my favorite time of day, my brother Peter's, too."

The words splintered the fragile pleasantries. Evening rose between them, swallowing up the waning daylight.

Cooper ground his teeth. Ruby was charming and lovely, but how could he have forgotten for a moment that the woman walking along beside him had accused his brother of child abduction, saddled Peter with an onerous sentence that would weigh down his soul with endless sorrow?

Ruby said Peter was in the woods that day and she saw him there, crouching behind the bushes, watching them. Peter maintained he was not anywhere near the two girls the morning Alice disappeared. So who was telling the truth? A five-year-old girl who had seen Peter many times in those very woods? Or Peter, a fifteen-year-old boy who was supposed to be sweeping floors at the lumber mill but hadn't shown up for work that day?

Ruby was just a child at the time, like Alice, he reminded himself.

But Peter was just a kid, too.

He slowed his pace and allowed Ruby to catch up while he breathed in the comfort of the forest, letting it soothe the angry thoughts away. Though he was loathe to do it, he forced some conversation to ease the distance he'd created between them. "The Umatilla National Park, where I work when I'm not on loan here, is thinking of thinning a stand of ponderosa pines to open up the canopy a bit. I've been doing the botanical surveys."

Ruby nodded. "Find anything interesting?"

"A new species of wild carrot," he said, glancing at her sideways. "You actually look interested. Most people put me into the crazy-plant-guy category when I tell them about the carrots."

She sighed. "I'm in the crazy-bird-gal category so I guess I can sympathize. I wish I could explain it better to folks. It's just that everything here makes sense, you know? Things live and die, sometimes so quietly we never even know they existed."

He took her hand when she stumbled over a twisted log crossing the path. Instinct, he told himself, though he could not explain why her touch made his nerves jump. "Maybe that's why you and

I do what we do, right? To take notice. To record that quiet life."

Her fingers felt very small and cold in his palm.

"I wish someone had recorded what happened to Alice. If only somebody knew."

He squeezed her hand and watched the last light imprint sparks deep down in her irises. The words flowed out. "I'm thinking it will all come out, maybe soon."

"Do you believe that?"

He smiled, and found he could answer truthfully. "Yes, I do. Maybe that's why the locket's turned up now."

She gripped his hand with sudden ferocity. "It's what I want, what I've always desperately wanted, but at the same time, it scares me."

And way deep down, where the roots of his soul were anchored, it scared him also. He started to respond when a squeal caught his attention, the echoing sound of a window closing or a stubborn sliding door being wrenched ajar.

"Up that way," he pointed. "Isn't that where the Walkers used to live?"

"Josephine still does." Yet they both knew Josephine was in the hospital.

He headed up a steep slope where there was barely a trail to be followed. Hardly a challenge for a guy who bushwhacked his way through acres of wilderness on a regular basis. Ruby, he noted, must have done her share of bushwhacking, too, as she stayed at his heels this time until they crested the slope together.

The Walkers' cabin sat at the bottom, a wood-sided structure with a sagging roof. The yard around the place was home to a car that appeared not to have run in a very long time and a set of tools laced with rust.

A light glowed in the front window, through a gap in the curtains.

"It must be Lester," Ruby said. "Alice was right, he really is home."

She started down the uneven path that served as a walkway.

"Is this a good idea?" Cooper asked.

"I just want to ask him if he saw the locket and make sure he knows his wife is in the hospital. He might not have heard about Josephine's stroke since he doesn't have a phone."

Cooper was never uncomfortable to be completely isolated, nor did he fear the darkness or anything in it, but something about the ramshackle house with the harsh light glaring through the curtains rattled him.

They hiked down, and Ruby knocked on the door. When no one answered, she called again. "Mr. Walker? It's Ruby Hudson. I have some information for you. Can we talk?"

Nothing stirred inside.

"Mr. Walker?" Ruby tried again.

Cooper leaned close and whispered, his lips touching the tender softness of her earlobe. "He doesn't want to talk to us. Let's go."

She shivered, perhaps from his whisper or the gathering cool of the evening, and followed him away. A moment later, they heard the squeal of the back sliding door.

Ruby set off in a jog. "I've got to tell him that locket has to go to the police."

"No," he called, but she trotted down the slope and disappeared through the densely clustered shrubs.

He followed after her, brushing aside the branches that obstructed his path. She stood, hands on hips, in the grass that had overtaken a broken birdbath filled with green water. "Where did he go?"

The sliding door was closed and Cooper peered into the darkened living room. "Seems like he could have just stayed inside and ignored us. No real reason to…" He felt a stirring in the air, a strange electricity that made him spin around.

Ruby stared at him with eyes round and terrified. A hooded figure wearing a bulky jacket embraced her from behind, one wiry arm around her shoulders and the other with a box cutter pressed to her neck, wicked steel against her creamy white throat.

FOUR

Ruby clung to the arm that circled her neck, feeling the hard muscles taut with anger and the edge of the blade pressing her windpipe. A man? A woman?

"Why are you here?" a voice whispered in her ear.

"I'm…" Ruby was too scared to push out any more words. She swallowed, trying again when Cooper stepped closer, palms up in a placating gesture. "Sorry if we scared you. We don't want to cause trouble. Just looking for Lester Walker. Is that you?"

A grunt.

Cooper nodded. "Okay. Your wife is in the hospital right now. We were coming to give you the message." He pointed to Ruby. "She was going to tell you. How about you let her go now?"

"How about," her attacker snarled, breath hot on her neck, "I cut her throat?"

Cooper moved closer, his tone harder now. "You don't want to do that. I understand you're upset. Our fault for trespassing. We'll take you to Josephine. No reason to hurt Ruby."

The arm tightened around Ruby's throat. "I think there's every reason."

"Lester, please. I know you suffered a terrible loss, but there's new evidence. This time we found her locket."

"Police and investigators can make evidence say whatever they want."

The stranger's grip tightened. Ruby struggled to breathe.

Everything happened in a blur. Cooper leaped forward. Lester loosened his hold a fraction, and Ruby stomped down hard on a foot. With a loud groan, Ruby was shoved forward into Cooper's chest and they went over backward onto the ground. She could hear Lester running away.

Ruby felt the breath explode out of Cooper as her elbow drove into his stomach. He rolled away and was on his feet in one fluid movement.

"No, Cooper. Don't go after him," she yelled, shoving the hair from her face and trying to scramble to her feet. By the time she did, Cooper was already gone, disappeared into the dark stand of firs.

She listened, hearing nothing but the wild beating of her own heart as it knocked into her ribs. A cold wind seemed to reach through her skin and chill her from the inside out. With shaking fingers, she picked up her cell phone. No signal. It shouldn't have surprised her. She moved to a spot farther away from the trees and managed to get a few bars and call 911.

When the dispatcher answered, she tried to corral her stampeding thoughts. "This is Ruby Hudson. A man, I think it was Lester Walker, attacked me with a knife on his property and…and Cooper Stokes took off after him."

No she wasn't hurt.

Yes, she was safe at the moment.

But what about Cooper?

She should go after him, but her brother would say summoning help was the most important task. Every minute wasted worsened the disaster.

Like every minute she'd spent calling for Alice that long-ago afternoon in the dark woods before she'd raced home to tell her family. Panic rose inside and she forced herself to talk slowly, though she wanted nothing more than to click off the phone and sprint after Cooper.

When she was through the litany of questions, she could stand no more. After promising the dispatcher she would head back to her house and wait for an officer, she pocketed the phone and made for the break in the trees. The sky was near black and the interlaced branches formed a living ceiling that crowded out the starlight. Pine needles cushioned her steps. She bit back a scream as a figure stepped through a gap in the branches. Cooper.

"It's you," she said, stupidly.

He did not seem injured, just winded. "Whoever that was, knows the woods better than I do. Lost me easily when the sun set. Runs like a deer."

"It had to have been Lester." Ruby put her hands on her hips. "Why did you do that? Run after him when he was obviously disturbed? That was crazy."

Cooper blinked. "He held a blade to your throat."

"And getting yourself stabbed would have erased that somehow?"

He moved close, his eyes gleaming silver in the gloaming. "Blade," he repeated slowly, "to your throat."

The fire in his eyes awakened a strange warmth in her body. Blood pounded through her veins, sending tingles through her stomach. "Misplaced gallantry." Gallantry she did not deserve nor want.

"Not gallantry." His shadow mingled with hers. "Justice."

"There isn't any justice, Cooper." Her voice sounded so breathy and sad, she almost didn't recognize it. "Haven't you learned that by now?"

"Sometimes there is, Ruby, but it's a long time in coming." He reached out, and she held her breath as he plucked a twig from her hair and sent it floating to the ground.

Tears crowded her eyes. "After what happened to Alice and Peter, you should know better."

"Whoever took Alice will get his punishment

eventually. I'm just hoping I can do my bit to set things right now. If that means I have to step up and chase a crazy old guy now and then, I'm game for the challenge."

He reached for her and his palms grazed her shoulders so tenderly, so tentatively, it weakened her.

"Cooper," she breathed. "You scared me."

"I'm honored that you care." He trailed his fingers through her hair.

"I don't…" She wanted to push closer, to keep him close, to trust him. Panic prickled her skin. She could not allow the strange thud of weakness to undo her. She jerked away. "What if you learn it was your brother who took Alice?"

He stiffened. "I won't, because he didn't."

"You can't know that."

"I know my brother like you know yours."

Pine needles drifted in the breeze, coming to rest at her feet. She was suddenly bone weary. "Sheriff's people are going to meet me back at the house. You'd better come, too."

He stopped her with a hand on her arm. "One thing." He tipped her chin back and leaned close.

Her eyes closed as his breath played over her neck. "Wanted to be sure he didn't cut you."

"I'm okay," she said, but she could feel her knees trembling. From his touch? Or the aftermath of Lester's rage? She was not sure as they picked their way through the trees.

Cooper answered all Sheriff Pickford's questions as did Ruby until it was nearly ten o'clock and he could no longer suppress a yawn. Pickford promised to have his people find Lester Walker and bring him in.

"He'll come back to the house sooner or later and we'll get him. In the meantime, we'll search the house for the locket." Pickford eased his bulk out of the kitchen chair. "Need a ride back to your cabin, Cooper?"

"No, thanks. I'll walk."

Ruby shot him a look. "What if Lester is still out there and he finds you?"

"I'll win him over with my easygoing charm." Cooper enjoyed her exasperated eye roll.

"He has a knife."

"A box cutter, actually," Cooper said, "and I'm scrappy. I'm pretty sure I can take him."

That elicited a laugh from Mick. "You would have made a good marine with that attitude."

It wasn't exactly a compliment, but at least Mick didn't look murderous. Then again, why should he care? Mick would be thrilled to pin Alice's disappearance on Peter. *Not gonna happen, Hudsons.*

Cooper watched Perry, who was silently sipping

a cup of coffee. He had tracked every syllable of the police questioning without comment. Now his eyes shifted in thought. When he felt Cooper's gaze on him, he offered a small smile.

"Mr. Hudson, do you know something about Lester Walker?"

Perry regarded Cooper calmly. "If I knew anything that would be of help, I would mention it."

Pickford looked up from his notebook, eyes narrowed. "How about sharing everything, and I'll decide if it would be helpful."

Perry's voice did not increase in volume, but it seemed to Cooper that the tension kicked up a notch. "My daughter was attacked, Sheriff. I've got every reason to cooperate." He smiled. "No hidden secrets here. You know what I know."

Pickford did not look convinced. Cooper wasn't either. He wanted to push harder, to get past the sanctimonious surface of this perfect family patriarch. Instead, he excused himself, suddenly desperate for the solace of the forest. Ruby watched from the door as he left, so he gave her a wink and a jaunty wave. Mick put an arm on her shoulder and guided her back into the house. *Keep away from Cooper and his brother,* the gesture said. *They're bad people.*

The injustice of it burned in him afresh. It had been a mistake to return to Silver Peak to check on the brother who he'd come to learn could not be saved by fraternal love. But that stubborn something rumbled inside him, that raw aching need to believe that maybe this time, unlike the hundred times before, would be the moment when Peter really did beat his addiction once and for all and grab hold of the life he had left.

But here in this small town would be the hardest place in the universe for Peter to face down the shadows of his past now that Alice Walker's case had been reopened. Then again, maybe it was the only place where he would truly know he'd beaten back the darkness.

Cooper let himself into the dusty cabin. He called for his brother and once again received no reply. The night chill had crept in. The place offered only a stone fireplace for warmth and it was late to start a fire, but he trudged out to the woodpile anyway, the feverish energy inside his body telling him there would be no sleep forthcoming. Might as well warm up the place. Besides, the cramped space aggravated his claustrophobia.

There was no kindling that he could find, so he put the axe to use and split more logs than he could possibly need into small pieces. It felt good to swing the heavy blade. The motion soothed him, the way the axe reduced the mammoth mound of wood into manageable units. With an armful of kindling and a couple of gnarled logs, he headed back, picking his way along the moonlit path that he and his father had graveled over one unusually warm Oregon summer. He'd much rather have been out exploring the woods or eating ice cream in town, but as his father said, "Take care of family first."

He shot a look at the vast dome of sky above him. *I'm trying, Dad.*

Each crunch of the gravel underfoot echoed with his father's admonition and he wondered for the millionth time if he had done enough to care for Peter. Or, as he'd learned over the years, had he done too much? Encouragement and enabling were perilously close.

He shifted the wood in his arms to free up a hand to shove the door open. He was startled to find it already was. Had he left it ajar and the wind took it? Or could it be his prodigal brother who'd finally seen fit to return?

Could be either, but there was also Lester Walker to consider. Cooper eased the pile of wood down on the spongy ground and extracted one slender log from the jumble. Club-size, about eighteen inches long. Enough to protect himself against a box cutter if the easygoing-charm thing didn't work out.

He pushed the door open with a foot. The interior was dark except for the light he'd left on in the kitchen. He eased inside.

"Peter?"

A figure emerged from the kitchen.

"Couldn't have been more wrong," he muttered, as the cabin lights snapped on and dazzled his vision.

FIVE

"You can put down the log," a woman said with a smile. She wore a long jacket, her auburn hair pulled back in a messy ponytail. "I'm not going to hurt you. I'm Heather Bradford."

He recognized her as the reporter outside the police station after Josephine had her stroke. "You're just here to burgle the place?"

A small, clean-shaven man with a thatch of dark hair stepped out of the kitchen. He was trim, in good shape, with the muscled body of a long-distance runner. "She didn't break in. The door was open."

"I forgot how relaxed the visiting policies are here in Oregon. If the door's open, just invite yourself in and set a spell." Cooper tossed the log he was holding into the fireplace. "Mind telling me who you are?"

"Hank Bradford, Heather's father. I try to accompany her on these investigative missions. Can't be too careful." His eyes swept over Cooper. "Never know about folks."

"Says the man standing in my cabin uninvited."

"Sorry about that," Heather said. "It was my idea to come. I knew you were staying with Peter for a while. You refused to talk to me via the phone. Thought I might persuade you in person."

"How exactly did you know I was staying with Peter?"

"You two don't talk much, I guess," Heather said, with a sideways grin. "Peter and I connected a few months back. We're friends, close friends. He works for my Dad."

"I own a small café in Pine Cliffs," Hank offered. Breakfast and lunch. Everything made from scratch and a new menu every day. Heather convinced me to hire Peter."

"And why would you do that, exactly?" Cooper demanded. "Hire my brother, I mean?"

"I was a manager at the Spruce Lodge here in town years ago when you two were kids. Peter washed dishes there in the summers, so we knew each other."

Cooper finally remembered.

Hank looked away for a moment before finishing. "Frankly, I always felt kind of sorry for Peter, being accused of that terrible crime. He was just a kid himself. Wrong place at the wrong time."

"You were here when Alice was abducted?"

"Close. Had a small place couple towns over in the woods. Real quite and no neighbors. I ran the breakfast service for the Lodge. I was part of the search party that looked for Alice."

"So you believe my brother is innocent?"

"Of course we do," Heather answered.

Cooper thought he caught a quick flash of emotion in Hank's eyes. He believed in Peter enough to give him a job, but Hank didn't want his daughter making any kind of deep connection with Peter. Charity was one thing, watching your daughter seek out an alcoholic formerly accused of kidnapping was another. Frankly, Cooper would probably feel the same way if he were Hank.

"Heather, you're not here as a friend. You're looking to dig up a story, but that story brings my brother nothing but pain."

She put her hands in her pockets. "Maybe things have changed. Maybe now the new developments will bring him vindication."

"Somehow, I don't think that's your reason for digging into this, is it?"

She perched on the arm of the worn sofa. "Well yes, I'd be lying if I said it wouldn't be a great story to tell and help my career along. It's been on my back burner for a while but now that it's almost the twenty-year anniversary…"

Cooper felt sickened. As if it was some sort of event that should be trotted out to sell papers.

Hank put a hand on her shoulder. "It's my fault. After I moved away, it upset Heather's mother to hear about it so I didn't say much. Every so often the police would have a stab at solving it again and one time they came to interview me. She overheard. I told them I'd always thought Peter got the short end of the stick."

"So who do you believe did it?"

He and Heather exchanged a look.

Heather nodded at her father.

"Hudsons are covering up the truth," Hank said. "I've always thought so."

Heather nodded. "And I'm going to prove it, now that the locket's been found."

Cooper's mind raced. Peter was innocent, he knew it in his bones. But the Hudsons guilty of hiding the truth? He didn't believe it, yet there was the inexplicable tension between Pickford and the senior Hudson. And Mick had been questioned by the police about Alice's disappearance, too. Was it possible?

"You don't think it might have been Lester Walker?" Peter said.

Hank shrugged. "Dunno, but they checked him out thoroughly. He was buying some parts for his truck in Forestville when it happened, I think I remember. He loved his kid, from what I hear."

"Where is Peter now?"

"At the café," Heather said. "He's worked some really long shifts and volunteered for extra hours. We have a small room in the back with a cot and he crashes there sometimes. He said he would head home after he got some shut-eye."

Relief washed through him. It was a lot better than the scenarios he'd been cooking up in his mind. He wanted them to depart, to leave him in peace so he could crank up the jazz music, pace the cabin floor all night. He caught Heather's eye and held it. "Look, I'll think about it and give you a call, but I'm going to ask you flat out to leave Peter alone about this situation. You know he's an alcoholic; I don't want his sobriety threatened."

Heather stood and raised her chin. "If I'm right, the truth will finally exonerate him. He will be able to look everyone in this town right in the eye and say, 'You were wrong about me.' That's the one thing he's craved all these years, isn't it?"

Cooper didn't answer.

She locked eyes on his. "He's yearned for the truth to come out, that he's not a child abductor or worse, and he's tried to drown that yearning in booze."

"It's more complicated than that."

"Yeah? Well I think the truth will set Peter free. Are you prepared to stand in the way of that?"

He stared into the flat blue of her eyes. Was he? Was protecting his brother also keeping the truth about Alice shrouded in darkness?

"I'd like you to leave now," he said. "Both of you."

She nodded. "All right, but I'll be back."

He waited until they were gone before he set a match to the dry wood and blew on the tiny flame until the wood caught. The warmth seemed infinitesimal to dispel the cold that gripped him.

Jazz. He needed some jazz. Thinking music. He thumbed through his iPod to find some Charlie Parker tunes that would sooth him into a place where he could make some decisions.

It was a good two hours later when the door swung open to admit his brother.

"Coop," Peter said, arms full of paper bags. "I'm home."

Cooper performed the first action automatically, scanning his brother's face, checking for the slack look, the bleary eyes, the aroma of alcohol as his brother put down the bags and grabbed him in a bear hug. When there were no indications that Peter had been drinking, Cooper felt the wash of guilt for his lack of trust. Would it always be like that? Distrust, guilt, disappointment? False hope? A real chance of healing? He let it go and returned his brother's embrace.

"I was expecting you yesterday."

Peter nodded, the dark blond hair grown long enough to touch his shoulders, deep creases on his tanned face. "Been working extra shifts at the café. Got dishpan hands, but earned some extra cash to get my car some new tires."

"I got a visit from Heather. She told me you were working at her dad's café."

"Yeah. Cool that he gave me a job. Don't exactly have much to offer in the way of work history on a resume."

"Peter, we need to talk."

"Right," his brother said, heading into the kitchen. "Can I cook while we talk? I'm starving."

Cooper watched as Peter moved around the kitchen. He was thin, maybe a bit too thin, but his hands were steady and sure as he minced garlic and chopped herbs to sprinkle on a pair of pork chops he'd fished out of the bag. Peter was an excellent cook, no doubt about that. "This place is a wreck, Coop." He heated olive oil and slid the meat into a pan. "If you're gonna stay with me, you'll have to learn to clean up after yourself."

Cooper was about to fire off a retort when he saw the grin. Typical Peter. The jokester. But the hunted look he'd seen in the past on his brother's face was no joke. He was relieved there was no sign of it now.

"Something has come up."

"Heard a few things. Why don't you tell me what you're worrying about? You get this crinkle between your eyebrows when you're stewing and it's gonna ruin your handsome baby face."

"It's coming up again, what happened to Alice all those years ago. I'm not sure it's a good idea for you to stay here."

Peter hesitated for a moment, staring into the sizzling pan. "I don't have anywhere else to go. Need to work. Can't stay with Mom, she's barely making it with the money you send her, and I know when I'm there she feels like she has to take care of me."

A thrill went through him at the unselfish words. *They're just words, Coop. He's got to walk the walk, not just talk about it.* Cooper took a deep breath. "Ruby Hudson found Alice Walker's locket hanging in a tree."

Peter still did not look at Cooper. "I heard."

"You did?"

"Yeah. It means they can find the guy who snatched her. That's what you're thinking, right?"

The pop of oil startled Cooper, but Peter didn't flinch.

"Yes, but it's going to bring up a lot of bad blood."

"I'm tougher than I was when I was a teen, Coop."

Cooper waited. His brother had something to say.

Peter slowly turned to face him. "Are you worried that I'll be proven innocent?" Another hiss and pop from the hot oil. "Or guilty?"

Cooper gaped. "You're a piece of work to say that after I've stood by you since the moment it happened. I know you'll be proven innocent."

"You're a better brother than I deserve."

Something flickered across Peter's face for a split second. In that tiny increment of time, Cooper's soul quaked. "Peter, I know you didn't do anything to

Alice Walker and you've told the police everything about that day."

Peter looked away, fussing over the dinner.

Peter was innocent.

Wasn't he?

Ruby sat bolt upright in bed. No sunlight peeked through a gap in the curtains yet. The thought that had niggled at her since she found the locket burst into her consciousness with crystal clarity. The clock read four-thirty. Her brother and father were still asleep, but she could not stow the idea churning through her mind a moment longer.

Throwing on a pair of jeans and a thick sweater that had been a gift from Molly Pickford on Ruby's high school graduation day, Ruby tiptoed into the kitchen, filled her thermos with coffee, snatched up her cell phone and tossed them both into a backpack before padding outside. She retrieved her hiking boots from the porch and laced them on. A thrill of fear rippled through her. Lester, if it really was him, was still at large somewhere, but she did not think he would brave the sanctuary property, and definitely not with the police on the lookout for him.

Still, anxiety lingered in her veins, but she forced herself into action anyway. Her whole life had been steeped in fear that colored and shadowed every moment since Alice disappeared, and she was sick of it. Finally, it seemed, there was a chance to shed some light in that darkness, and she would not let the precious moment pass. She'd have to be certain before she told anyone else.

Jacket zipped and cell phone clutched in her hand, she headed out. The sky was unclouded, which meant precisely nothing on the southern coast of Oregon. A lovely morning could morph into a rainy afternoon. Overhead the sounds of rustling birds reminded her that life was burgeoning again as spring meant babies for many species. Her precious bald eagles were tending to their young eaglets, the awkward fuzzy creatures not yet ready to fly. They needed constant attention, which they received from both the mother and father.

An image of her mother rose in her mind, a photo she'd seen of an elegantly dressed, smiling woman holding court at a Hudson family Christmas party in their neat San Francisco Victorian. Ruby had no memories of her mother that weren't secondhand stories told by her father or Mick. As a young child, she'd thought about those anecdotes, embroidered them in her mind, hoping to embed them so deep they would somehow become her own, but they hadn't. Ruby had no imprint of her mother, like a bird abandoned just after hatching. If things had been different, and her mother had not succumbed to the cancer, would she have let Ruby go into the woods that day with Alice? Or might they never have come to Oregon at all, staying in San Francisco, amid the forest of eclectic buildings instead of the whispering pines?

She had almost reached the tree when she heard footsteps running through the underbrush, moving fast, coming close. She slipped behind a screen of bushes, heart thudding. Thoughts of Josephine's knife slicing into her flesh and Lester's hot breath against her throat ratcheted her pulse even faster.

Stay hidden. You're safe.

Not in these woods, her mind taunted.

Not anywhere.

Cooper burst into view, his sweatshirt damp with perspiration, moving fast and fluid as he churned along the path. The intensity in his face brought her to her feet, and before she thought it through she'd stepped out of her concealment.

He jerked to a stop, breathing hard, sweat glistening on his face. "Ruby," he panted. "What are you doing out here at this hour?"

She wished now she'd stayed hidden. "I was, uh, checking on something. Do you always run before sunup?"

He shrugged. "Couldn't sleep. Insomniac. It's either run or watch countless hours of NBA basketball reruns." He paused. "My brother's home."

"Oh. I'm glad he made it." The silence grew awkward between them. She wished he would say goodbye and move on, leave her to her mission. He didn't, staying there with hands to his narrow waist, regarding her without his usual good-natured smile, which made her wonder.

"I heard from the sheriff that there was no sign of the locket at the Walker's house."

"Hmmm. That's a setback. So what are you checking out then?"

She sighed. No point in holding back. "I just wanted to see if my memory was accurate." The pine needles under the tree were thick and fragrant as she knelt and sifted her fingers through the detritus.

He took a knee next to her, uncomfortably close, heat emanating from his body. He didn't say anything, which made her feel a pressing need to fill the silence.

"When I found it, the necklace I mean, some debris from the nest fell down. I didn't think anything of it at the time. The nest has been vacant for years. As the trees grew up around this one, it obscured the view, you see, and eagles don't like to have their view obstructed so they found another location. The tree sort of became invisible until the others around it were cleared."

He let her babble, crouched down, one arm resting on his muscular thigh. When she ran out of breath, he nodded. "So what are we looking for?"

"This," she said, snatching up the fragment and holding it up to the light.

He squinted. "Looks like part of a fish backbone."

"It is. Amazing that it's still intact, but it was tucked between the twigs, which sheltered it from the elements, I think. The rest just sort of disintegrated. There are really only a few vertebrae left."

"You're the bird expert and all, I'm just a plant guy, but isn't it pretty common to find fish remnants in an eagle's nest? They're really into seafood, right?"

She smiled. "Sure, but it got me to thinking about how the locket got up into the tree. It couldn't have been carried by the wind and eagles aren't like magpies that collect every shiny thing they see, so how did it get in the nest? It's possible it was tangled in a branch that one of them brought to the nest, I suppose, but I came up with this crazy notion that it got here…"

His eyebrows shot up. "Via the fish."

"Exactly." She was pleased that she did not see disbelief in his look. "The eagle carried the fish up here and the necklace was inside the fish's stomach."

He laughed. "I believe it. My brother and I once caught a salmon with a watch in its stomach. Fish gobble first and think about it later."

"Right. When the eagle tore away the flesh, the locket fell out and got caught in the branches."

"Which means," he said, standing and offering her a hand, helping her to her feet, "that someone chucked the necklace in the lake to get rid of it, but your eagle friend brought it back here."

"Ironic, don't you think?"

"Amazing, is more like it. After twenty years, long after the fish and eagle are gone, Ruby Hudson happens along and finds it. What a break."

She winced. "I don't believe in breaks anymore."

He brushed pine needles off of his knees. "I do." His smile faltered. "And I wouldn't say no to one that helped solve Alice's disappearance."

"What did Peter have to say about the locket?"

"Not much." His mouth tightened. "He was exhausted so I didn't get a chance to tell him about Lester. He's been working hard."

Something in his voice was uncertain, wary perhaps?

Cooper straightened. "I'll go change and fill him in. Then we can head out."

"Head out?"

"Are you a runner?"

"Not unless something's on fire."

He grinned. "Okay. I'll hold myself back to a brisk walk. Let's go. I need to get out of these sweaty clothes before we leave." He charged off.

"Leave for where?" she called, scrambling to catch up with his long-legged strides.

"You're planning on going to the lake, aren't you?"

How had he known that was her plan? To go to the lake, by herself.

"There's no point, really. After twenty years there is nothing left there that will show us what happened to Alice."

"Well, we just figured out whoever had her locket was probably there twenty years ago, and that's more than we've known until this moment. Gotta go and see if we can figure out anything, right? Reconstruct the scene? Make like detectives?"

"Okay," she said, weakly, mulling in her mind how her plan had suddenly come to include Cooper. "But it's really going to be a waste of time. I can go by myself, no need for you to…"

Cooper disappeared around a bend in the path, leaving her talking to herself.

SIX

Peter was padding out of the kitchen with a coffee mug clutched in his hand when they arrived. His hair stood up in unruly tufts, and he looked as though he'd slept in his clothes, but Cooper didn't care. As long as Peter was sober, he could dress however he wanted.

Cooper introduced Ruby, but there was no need.

"Yeah, I remember Ruby," Peter said. He kept his eyes on the rim of his mug as he drank. It was hard to decipher the tone in Peter's words. It wasn't quite anger or dismissal.

"Nice to have the cabin occupied again," Ruby said.

Peter nodded, checking his battered Timex. "Gotta get moving. Going to work today."

Cooper quashed the hopeful feeling before it could blossom. "Need a lift to town?"

"Nah. Car's still okay for a few more miles. I'll get new tires as soon as I get paid."

Cooper wanted to interrogate his brother about

their awkward conversation the prior evening, and many other things, but instead he quickly changed into jeans and a T-shirt while Peter turned back to the kitchen for more coffee. Peter did not offer any to Ruby so Cooper did, but she declined, sitting stiffly on the couch as Cooper laced his shoes. "We're heading to the lake to check on something."

"Related to Alice Walker?"

"Not sure, but there's something else I meant to tell you." Cooper recapped the encounter with Lester Walker as briefly as possible for his brother. He kept it factual, leaving out the horror he'd experienced at seeing the box cutter pressed to Ruby's throat since he still hadn't had a chance to sort through his own muddled emotions about it. "So if you see him, call the sheriff's office. Do you have a cell phone?"

Peter stared at him, face white. "What?"

"I asked if you have a cell phone?"

"No, what you said before. About Lester."

"We think he's the guy who attacked Ruby at the Walker cabin."

"No." Peter shook his head, splashing coffee onto the floor. "No, it couldn't have been Lester Walker."

Again the feeling of dread sprang up inside. Cooper restrained himself from exchanging a look with Ruby. "Why do you say that?"

Peter blinked. "I, what I meant was, Lester beat

it out of town a long time ago. He wouldn't have come back."

"You did," Ruby said. "So why not Lester?"

He put the mug in the sink. "Dunno. I was just surprised, is all. That he would return, I mean, when there's nothing here for him."

"Josephine's still here," Ruby said, quietly. "And she needs him now more than ever."

"Yeah. Sure. I see your point. Gonna go shower before I head to town."

Cooper walked Ruby outside and pulled the door closed. Her frown told him she thought Peter's reaction was odd. The instinct to defend kicked up.

"He's adjusting to the circumstances, to having all this brought up again."

"He seemed certain that Lester couldn't have returned."

"Like I said, he's got a lot to adjust to." He read the question in her eyes. "He's sober," he snapped, "if that's what you're thinking."

She flinched. "I never implied that he wasn't. It's a long hike. We'd better get started."

He let her walk a couple of yards ahead of him, letting the anger die down as his better instincts took over and he jogged to catch up. "Hey, I'm sorry. I'm so used to defending my brother, I do it even when he isn't under attack."

She didn't look at him. "Don't be too sorry, because I actually was wondering if Peter was sober."

Cooper sighed. The spark of anger faded into a dull throb of pain. "I wonder all the time, too. I can't imagine what it would feel like to trust that he'd truly beaten back the alcoholism. So many times I believed him and every single time he let me down. No, he let himself down." It hurt to say it, but taking off his armor for a moment helped.

"That's a hard situation, a difficult way to grow up."

"He's my brother, and I love him."

She reached up on tiptoe and hugged him. She was so delicate, the top of her head reaching just under his chin, her arms twining around his neck. Instinctively, he returned the embrace, warmth speeding through his body, marveling at the softness of her and the comfort he felt with her pressed against him. As she released him, he could see she was surprised at her own impulsiveness. Her cheeks pinked. "You're a good brother to Peter."

Guilt flamed anew. Would a good brother have suspicion slithering through his belly? He stepped back. "Sometimes, I'm not so sure."

They took a brisk pace through the forest, the newly risen sun dappling them in gold. His spirits rose, as they always did when he submerged himself in God's spectacular creation. He tried to keep his mind on the array of wild grasses and tree species, mentally comparing them to the botanical variety in his stomping grounds in the Umatilla.

They followed the edge of a brush field, abutted on one side by a road that marked the eastern border of the sanctuary property, and on the other, by a dense tangle of shrubbery where a rough-hewn trail promised a route to Sunstone Lake.

As they took in the sweep of grass and flowering shrubs, he found himself reaching for the iPad, which, of course, he'd left at the cabin.

"Something caught your eye?" Ruby teased.

He grinned. "There."

Ruby peered around in confusion until he moved her close and they squatted in front of an elaborately petaled red flowering plant.

"Western lily. They're endangered." He took out his cell phone and clicked a series of pictures. "Awww, man. I would give my eye teeth for something to take notes on."

"No need to sacrifice your teeth. Here." She handed him a spiral notebook and a stubby pencil. He planted a courtly kiss on her hand.

She laughed. "You are easy to please."

He scribbled notes about the lily and the surrounding plants.

"The position of the stamens and presence of the green star distinguish it from the *pardalinium*." He looked up at the sound of her laughter. "Uh-oh. Plant geek on the loose."

The sunlight caught the brilliance of her smile and the spangle of freckles on her luminous skin.

"I'm happy to have a fellow geek to talk to. I can go on for days about peregrine falcon taxonomy."

He was riveted by her eyes, filled with passion for her subject as he knew his own to be, brimming with life. She shone with the same fresh perfection of a new bloom. It took him a while to realize he was staring, so he shook himself back to reality. He was scribbling some meaningless notes to cover his discomfort when a small red pickup came around the turn in the road, moving fast. Behind it raced the sheriff's official car.

The pickup showed no sign of stopping until the sheriff blared his horn. Then it lurched to a halt, and the driver's door slammed open. Molly Pickford got out and stood, hands on hips in the middle of the road.

"Stop treating me like a criminal, Wallace," she yelled. "I've had enough."

Sheriff Pickford heaved himself out. At this distance, his features were not clear, but Cooper could tell by the body language that the man was furious.

Cooper looked at Ruby. It was not a scene they were meant to overhear and he felt like an eavesdropper, but there was such rage in the sheriff's approach, Cooper feared for Molly's safety. He took a step closer.

Ruby gripped Cooper's arm, and he put a hand over hers.

Molly stood close to her husband. "If you don't trust me, that's your problem. Not mine."

"Trust? We had that twenty years ago, remember? And you broke it?"

She slapped a hand on her thigh. "I've tried to make it up to you, to show you that was a mistake and it won't happen again. I've done everything I can to make up for what I did. When will I be forgiven, Wallace?"

"Maybe when you stop running off to see other men at every opportunity. Where have you been? Hanging out at a certain diner, maybe, now that he's back in town?"

"I'm not even going to answer that. You know that was over a long time ago."

"And what about your other gentleman friend? You see him on a regular basis."

"I drop in sometimes, because we're friends. That's what friends do. If you had any, you'd know that."

"I have a wife, and she's supposed to be my best friend."

"Well maybe it's time for you to get a new wife, Wallace, because clearly I don't fit the bill."

He took a step forward and Cooper tensed. "I'm going to let them know we're here," Cooper whispered, but Pickford's next words left him frozen to the spot.

"You won't leave me, Molly. Not for him, not for any man."

"You don't own me," she said.

Pickford's voice dropped to a lower range, something plaintive in the words. "What does he have? What makes him so attractive, Moll?"

"I told you, he's just a friend, but he trusts me to make the right decisions. I wish you did the same. Now unless you're going to arrest me, I'm going to go back home and take a walk."

"Alone?"

Without answering, she whirled on her heel and got back into the pickup, driving away at a good clip.

Pickford stared after her for a while. He kicked the door of his car with such force his booted foot dented the metal. Ruby let out a cry, hand tightening on Cooper's arm. Pickford heard it. He stared in their direction for a moment before turning, and wrenching open the door. He spun the car into a messy turn and roared off.

"Do you suppose he saw us?" Cooper noticed Ruby looking not at the retreating police car, but in the direction Molly had taken. "What do you make of that?"

Ruby chewed her lip. "Pickford thinks his wife is having an affair. Apparently she had one before, years ago, and now that she's friends with another man, Pickford can't stand it."

"This 'friend' better watch his back. Who do you think it is?"

Ruby continued to stare after the departed pickup, her eyes round and fearful. "My father."

Ruby was grateful that Cooper remained in shocked silence for a few beats while she collected herself. She had not realized until just that moment how Molly's friendship with her father played into the larger picture. Molly had been a huge help to Perry after they moved to Silver Peak, especially in matters where a woman's touch was required. Molly helped Ruby buy a homecoming dress, comforted her when her various high school loves had dumped her.

"She brings cookies every so often," Ruby mused aloud. "Chocolate chip, my father's favorite."

Cooper didn't say anything.

"It's not an affair," she hastened to add. "They're friends. Dad's supported Molly and offered her advice sometimes, but that's as far as it goes. My brother said she was in bad trouble a long time ago, and Dad helped her out. Just good friends."

"Pickford seems to think otherwise."

Ruby's stomach tightened as she recalled a scene from the past when Pickford had shown up and gotten into a shouting match with her father. Mick had joined their father, shoulders squared and hands in fists. Ruby remembered thinking how big her brother looked then, as he squared off against Pickford.

She'd heard only one bit of the encounter.

"…thrown in jail," Pickford had bellowed.

She'd wondered then as she wondered now. Was it Mick he'd threatened with jail? Or her father? She shook away the memory and focused on Cooper. "Really, I'm telling you my father would not have an affair with a married woman."

"I know you believe that."

Her jaw tightened. "But you don't? You think he's that kind of man?"

He folded his arms. "I don't know your father at all. And recently I've heard…"

"Heard what?"

"Nothing. You know your father and you trust him. Does it matter what I think?"

For some reason that she could not fathom, it did matter what Cooper thought. "You're right, I know him better than you do."

"And you want me to believe in him, Ruby, just like we wanted your family to believe in my brother, but you didn't." He flung an arm wide. "No one in this whole town did, except come to find out, Hank Bradford. Heather's father."

"What does he have to do with this?"

"Nothing much. One voice among hundreds." Cooper sighed and looked at the ground. "I guess the point is, it's hard for me to trust your family when you didn't trust mine."

"My father investigated. That's all."

Cooper stared sadly at her. "Investigated. And ordered his family to stay away. What did he tell you? If you see Cooper or Peter in the woods, come home immediately. Don't play with Cooper at school. Give the required level of courtesy and that's it. No more friendship."

Her stomach fell to her feet. "I never…"

But she had. A memory floated back to her, a young Cooper calling to her to see a bird's nest he'd located in a tall tree on the school playground. Cooper had taken to playing by himself after Alice disappeared. She'd assumed it was by choice, but maybe the other children's parents told their kids to stay away from him, too. On that day, his face lit up as she started toward him, then crumbled as she remembered her father's warnings and she turned away, like all the other kids had.

"He was protecting me," she whispered.

"And you think a seven-year-old kid would see it that way?"

A breeze caught some fallen leaves and sent them cartwheeling on the wind. "I'm sorry, Cooper." Tears pricked her eyes. "Truly, I am sorry I hurt you. I never meant to." On impulse she embraced him and kissed his cheek, allowing her lips to trail over his tanned skin. She felt him shiver, a ripple that passed through his body into hers. "I'm so sorry."

"I know." He buried his head in the hollow of her neck. "The person who took Alice hurt us all. I still struggle to let it go. You, too?" The last words were hoarse, whispered into her hair.

She nodded, throat thick. "I thought finding the locket would be a good thing at first, but now I'm not so sure."

He held her, long arms cradling her as her cheek found rest against his hard chest. "I believe this is all going to work out."

The steady beat of his heart seemed to slow her own hammering pulse as warmth trickled through her veins. "Will we get the answers we want, Cooper?"

His fingers slowed on her back. "They may not be the ones we want, but they're the ones we need."

SEVEN

Things were happening too quickly for Cooper's comfort. Every day he spent in Silver Peak seemed to plunge him deeper into the shadows of the past, and secrets flickered to life like the birds in the branches. He was simultaneously drawn to Ruby and repelled by the residual hurt and anger that lingered deep down within him. She represented a past so dark that it took every ounce of his faith to believe they would ever escape it.

The path down to the lake was steep, and they had to work hard to keep their footing in places where the ground was slick with mud. Didn't matter. Signs of spring burgeoned around him, as countless tiny green plants sprang to life on the edges of the path. Laboring next to Ruby, he could not hold back a chuckle.

"What?" she demanded.

"Just struck me as funny. You are constantly looking up and I'm perpetually looking down." Seeing her smile lifted something inside him.

"I'm looking for birds."

"And I'm looking for buds." He gestured upward. "Though you do have a pretty thriving community of fir and cedar, I noticed."

"And best of all," she said, voice dropping as they approached a massive pine, "the eagles are back."

He followed her gaze to a tree that stood sentinel away from the others on an impossibly rocky spit of land. An immense, conical-shaped nest stood out against the branches. They stopped to watch an eagle waddling gingerly around the nest.

"She's one of my favorites. We call her Sheila. She lost an eye to injury, but she's seen ten babies fledge over the years. Her mate arrives and adds sticks and such to the nest, but she doesn't like his style because after he leaves she redecorates. It's funny to watch."

"Eaglets in the nest now?"

She nodded. "One, I think. Most of the time if there are two, the stronger one will kill the other."

He whistled. "Not easy being an eagle."

She sighed. "True."

They walked by, taking pains to keep quiet, though Cooper figured the eagles would not be the least bit nonplussed by the clumsy humans some two hundred feet below.

The sun reached its full golden splendor as the trail led them to Sunstone Lake. Wind-teased ripples sparkled on the surface of the oval-shaped water ringed by a thick carpet of fir, cedar and pine. The lake bulged out into various inlets both large and small, concealed by dense groupings of trees, flanked on the far side by a rocky cliff. Clusters of birds floated on the surface and others he could not identify scuttled busily along the shore. A cacophony of bird conversation filled the air.

Ruby sighed with pleasure. "Spring is busy here. We're a prime stop on the Pacific Flyway."

He knew. The Pacific Flyway was a route for migratory birds in America. They traversed that great invisible path from Alaska to Patagonia, following the food, looking for places to spend the winter and raise their babies.

"Your guests are pretty predictable?"

"Some arrivals I can almost time down to the exact day. Others..." She broke off. "Did you hear that?"

He nodded. "Boat engine. Can barely make it out over this bird chatter. You allow fishing here?"

She shook her head. "The land is strictly private property, no public access, and we don't have docks. We don't own the north shore, though. We have sort of an informal agreement about that."

He gazed toward the far side of the lake, too distant to see clearly, inlets tucked away like long-kept secrets. "Who lives there?"

"The Pickfords, since before we arrived. We've never had any trouble. They know how important the springtime is for our birds," she said with a frown. "They wouldn't venture out on this side of the lake, not now."

The engine noise died away, but Cooper's uneasy feeling did not. He watched the progress of a bald eagle as it swooped from a tree branch toward the water. Heavy wings slowed the bird, shifting the headlong dive into a talons-first approach. Cooper saw the strong claws flex as the bird plucked a trout from the water, soaring back to its lofty perch, the entire intricate ballet over in fewer than sixty seconds.

He blinked and realized Ruby was watching him.

"Amazing, isn't it?" she said.

He exhaled long and slow. "Only God could make a living thing as incredible as that."

"I used to think so, too," she said. "But how...?" She looked away.

The need in her voice struck at him. "How what?"

She looked at him full on, challenge burning in her chocolate eyes, arms crossed around her body. "If He makes life, why doesn't He take care of it?"

He knew what she meant. A little child...a tiny vulnerable being, snatched away, helpless, like the fish. Alive and carefree one moment and then gone the next.

He chose his words carefully. "People have been trying to figure that out since the beginning of time.

Job got a whole book in the Bible, and he asked the same thing."

"And what did God answer?"

"That He loves us and He's God and we don't get to understand everything."

Ruby's eyes hardened. "That's not good enough."

He sighed. "I feel the same way sometimes, but I choose to trust Him."

She took a step back. "I don't. Not anymore."

He wanted to take her hand, to embrace her and ease away that stark, flat anguish in her voice, but she moved from him, scanning the wide expanse teeming with feathered life.

"I don't know why we came here." She gestured at the lake. "It doesn't even look the same after twenty years. The trees have thickened, and we've had various rockfalls that pinched off pockets of water so even the outline of the lake is different. How could we possibly find anything to help us figure out what happened to Alice?"

"One thing that hasn't changed too much is the highest point—that rock cliff, I'm thinking." Cooper pointed to an ash-colored cliff, triangular in shape, that loomed over the far side of the lake. "Let's get a bird's-eye view, shall we?"

She huffed. "For what purpose?"

"If nothing else, I could use the exercise."

"You just went running this morning."

"For your information, I intend to power down

some mint chip ice cream later today, so I've got to stay active." Again, he'd won a smile. "And besides, wouldn't you like to check out your nesting sites on the far shore?"

He saw the desire flare up in her eyes. "The rocks are unstable there. We've had some slides. Mick insists I go with an escort."

"How fortunate," he said, doffing an imaginary cap, "that your humble servant is here to escort you."

With the sound of her laughter dancing in his ears, they started off for the far side of the lake.

Even though Ruby knew it was an exercise in futility, she could not help but enjoy the hike. Cooper's all-inclusive knowledge of botany complemented her own bird compendium, and his enthusiasm fed her own. Now she saw the lake through different eyes, as if she'd been given a peek at the comprehensive botanical underpinnings that supported the thriving bird community. A bird geek and a plant nerd. What a perfect pair they would be if their past history wasn't such a disaster.

When they reached the tumbled rock pile at the bottom of the cliff, they slowed their pace. The sandstone bluff rose in glittering splendor, cracked and splintered by the elements. It had been a long time since Ruby had made the climb to the top and that had been a hurried trek with Mick. Something about the erratic wind, the rising walls of the cliff that muted the bird noises, made her uneasy. Mick seemed to enjoy scouting the cliff side for caves, which appeared and disappeared over time behind screens of shrubbery and falling rubble. When Alice was snatched they had brought search dogs that had scoured these very slopes without finding a trace of the child. But what if the spring rains had diluted the scent? Suppose she'd come, or been brought here, imprisoned in a rocky tomb, and the dogs and searchers had passed her by?

Ruby shivered.

"You all right?"

"Sure, of course." She moved by him, eager to get the climb over and done with. The sandstone afforded a smooth path in some spots and in others the grit left them scrambling for traction.

"Your brother was right about these paths," Cooper said. "He doesn't have time to take you here much?"

"No. He likes to be alone a lot now."

"Why? What changed?"

She sighed. What had changed and taken the light out of her brother's eyes? It was not something he would ever share, especially with Cooper, but she found herself wanting to tell him. "He was a parole officer and one of his cases went bad. Very bad. He blames himself." She hoped Cooper would not pry and he didn't.

"Nothing weighs heavier than guilt," he said quietly.

She believed it.

When they reached the top, she was panting. Cooper, she noticed, was not even breathing hard. They looked out over the panorama, the lake dotted with hungry birds, the trees so green they looked black and the luxury of a clear, sun-filled sky.

"Top-notch view," Cooper said. He took a pair of binoculars from his pack. "Let's see if we can reconstruct things. Whoever took Alice would have wanted to get off sanctuary property without attracting notice. Only direct route back to the main road was impacted by construction so they were flagging cars through one at a time. No one noticed a child of Alice's description or any strangers of note."

Ruby forced the words out. "He… They could have put her in the trunk and driven right by without anyone knowing."

"That's true. But let's say the stranger didn't leave that way. The other route would be to hike to the lake, use a boat or walk around to the other side and connect to the frontage road."

"I agree, and the police investigated all that, but who's to say he drove anyway? Maybe it wasn't preplanned. Some stranger was in the woods, took

Alice and—" she swallowed "—killed her. Left her hidden there."

Cooper's voice was kind. "The woods were searched pretty carefully, but it's possible. One thing we know is the guy was here, at the lake, and tossed Alice's locket in the water where it was possibly swallowed by the trout." He paused and she knew the horrible thought that dawned in his mind.

She took his hand. "They sent divers in and detection dogs. No sign of Alice in the lake."

He heaved out a breath and squeezed her hand. "Just her locket." He looked through the binoculars again and then handed them to her. "Take a look down there, at the bottom of that big fissure. Does that look like a cave to you?"

She focused the lenses. "Yes. It's almost completely eclipsed by the shrubbery. How did you ever spot it?"

He tapped a solemn finger to his temple. "Old eagle-eyed Cooper. I can spot a wood thrush at fifty paces."

"We don't have wood thrushes here."

"Well if one flies in, I'm going to be the first one to spot it." He put away the binoculars. "I say we hike over there and take a look." He gave her an uncertain glance. "If you want to stay here, I'll be right back. Trail is steep and gravelly. Easy to twist an ankle."

It wasn't why he was discouraging her. There

was a chance, the slimmest one, that inside the cave they would find the body of her friend. All the horror washed over her again. Had she searched long enough? Called loud enough? Peered under every thicket and behind each tree trunk? *Nothing weighs heavier than guilt.* The only chance she had to put down that ponderous burden was to find out what had really happened to Alice Walker.

"I'm going, too. What's the best way?"

He gave a slight nod, as if her response had not surprised him. "Single file. I'll go first. Got your phone?"

"Yes."

"Keep it handy. If you feel yourself start to slip, sit down."

"And what if that doesn't work?"

He grinned. "I'll catch you."

"As we both career down the side of the cliff together?"

"You're a pessimist." He edged between two huge boulders into the crevice that served as a path. The ground was littered with broken shards worn away from the parent rock that loomed above them.

Tree roots curved into view here and there, twisted into arcs like gnarled fingers groping for the light. The rock walls blocked the sun and chilled Ruby.

"Wait," she said softly.

Cooper stopped, some five feet below her on the path. "What?"

She pointed upward. "I thought I heard something."

They both listened, hearing nothing but the breeze rattling the needles of the twisted pine and the faint, faraway sounds of the birds. She shrugged and waved him on, a flush of embarrassment warming her cheeks. Her imagination was running wild again.

She focused on each step, avoiding the pockets of grit, turning sideways where the path became impossibly steep. Above her, silhouetted against a cornflower-blue sky, was a fringe of jagged rock, fastened together in impossible fashion.

A sound filtered down into the rocky chute where she stood.

Rock grating against rock. Her imagination, surely?

"Cooper?" she said, but her voice came out only as a whisper.

Her fingers pressed against the sandstone wall and deep down, like an erratic pulse, she felt the tremor of movement.

"Cooper?" she called, louder.

He heard her that time and turned, green-gold eyes wide with a question. Framed by the glittering mass around him, arms pressed on either side against rock as if he alone was holding back the crush of stone, her heart registered that he was breathtaking even as her brain screamed at what was about to happen.

"Cooper!"

His reply was swallowed up by the groan as the rocks above them let loose.

EIGHT

One moment the sun shone in a mellow slice through the crevice and the next, the sky was blotted out by an avalanche of rock and dirt. He heard Ruby's scream. He tried to get to her but the ground shook, upsetting his balance.

Rock fragments broke away, smashing against the walls and cracking apart, showering him with sharp pieces. One cut into his arm, as he threw up a hand to shield his face. He fought against the wave of debris, pushing upward, struggling. "Ruby!" he shouted over the roar. Was it her scream he heard or the cliff unloading itself around him?

The trembling ground knocked him to his knees and he found himself skidding downward, fingers clawing, gravel scraping the skin from his forearms and elbows. Rocks continued to thunder upon him as he slid. Tumbled this way and that, he lost all orientation, the view obliterated by a blanket of billowing dust. Finally, he crashed stomach first into a fixed boulder, which stopped his progress so abruptly that the breath was driven out of him.

He wasn't sure if the clamor was the blood rushing through his veins or the continuing rock slide. All he could do was turn his face toward the boulder, sucking in as much air as he could as the mass settled around him, pressing him closer and closer to the unyielding boulder.

The roar subsided into a softer noise, the slower rumble of smaller fragments and then the shower of tiny pebbles, like stony raindrops pattering down around him. He coughed, choking on air thick with dust, pressing his body against the boulder until the world stopped moving. After a couple of slow breaths, he dared open his eyes. A white-brown wall of rock pressed up against his face.

You're alive, Cooper. Time to take stock. Arms, legs, shoulders all seemed to be in the right places, and he was able to wriggle all fingers and toes. An urgent thought pushed through the thudding pain in his head.

He had to get to Ruby. He tried to shove away from the boulder.

The relief he'd felt a moment before evaporated as he realized in a rush of horror that he could not move. The falling rocks had piled up, trapping him in the small gap at the base.

A claustrophobic's nightmare. He fought down the panic. Deep breath, try again.

Using all his strength he braced himself and shoved his back against the pile. Useless. Heavy stones hemmed him in, and he could not gain the leverage to dislodge himself. Fighting a wave of panic, he prayed that Ruby had not been hurt in the rockfall. Why had he insisted they investigate in spite of Mick's warnings? He'd gotten himself into a mess. That was par for the course, but what had he done to Ruby? *Way to go, Cooper.*

He shouted her name. With his face pressed inches from a half-ton rock, he did not think the sound would carry. Phone. Sweat ran down his face as he squirmed and wriggled. Inch by painful inch, he eased the phone out of the pocket of his jeans and snaked it up his body. Sweaty fingers caused him to lose his grip to the shifting debris.

"No way. Not now." Clawing through the mess, he found it again and punched the buttons to summon help. How long would it take for rescuers to find Ruby? His stomach constricted. How much medical attention would she require?

Straining his neck to the snapping point he realized his phone was displaying a message. No available signal. He groaned.

Did anyone know they were here? His brother, but he had a long workday ahead. It could be hours before anyone realized Cooper and Ruby were missing.

Okay, Cooper. No help coming, it's just you, wise guy. What's your big plan now?

He wasn't going to have the strength to bust out of the rock pile in superhero fashion. Somewhere above his head, light filtered through the pile of rubble. In that direction was the sun. In that direction, he prayed, Ruby was alive and well.

The one thing Cooper had left at his disposal was tenacity. His father always told him strength was mental, not physical. Time to put that theory to the test. Letting out his breath to make himself as skinny as possible, he began to wriggle toward the light.

Ruby pressed herself into the smallest bundle she could manage, sheltering under a network of exposed roots that jutted from the cliff wall. She felt as if she was at the epicenter of a violent explosion. The tide of earth careened over her until what seemed like an eternity later, the cascade slowed. Gingerly she extricated herself from underneath the roots. Head spinning, she got to her feet, peering through the settling dust. Most of the rock flow had passed right on by, leaving the path looking much as it had before except for one thing—Cooper was gone.

Scrambling down the path, she screamed for him. Again and again, her voice rose in pitch. "Answer me, Cooper Stokes, right now."

"Here," a voice called. It was Heather's father, Hank.

His shocked face appeared, looking down from

the rocks above. Heather joined him a moment later, eyes round as silver dollars.

"Are you hurt?" Hank called out.

"N-no." Ruby tried to force her mouth into motion. "But Cooper was farther down the trail." She pointed.

Heather's cheeks went white. "We'll try to get down to you. Don't move."

They vanished, and she could hear scrambling feet. The oddity of it struck her then. Hank and Heather. Where had they come from? It didn't penetrate past her fear of what had happened to Cooper. She moved forward toward the bend in the trail where a giant boulder protruded from a pile of debris. Some of the rocks at the base were smashed into jagged bits by the force of the rockfall. They would have wrought the same damage on bones and flesh. Her heart hammered a frantic tempo against her ribcage.

The path ended abruptly at the foot of the boulder, choked off by the debris that had collected in the bottleneck. Hank and Heather loosed a small shower of gravel as they approached.

"I don't see him," Ruby said, her voice wobbling. "Wouldn't he answer, if he could?"

Hank held up a hand. "Let's spread out, a few feet apart. Everyone listen for any kind of sound. I assume you've tried your phone?"

Ruby started, incredulous that it had not occurred to her before. She grabbed her phone and found there was no signal, so she crouched down and strained to listen, calling again and again for Cooper.

"Wait," Heather whispered. "I thought I heard something."

The three of them froze. Something moved in the pile, a subtle shifting in the debris.

"There." Ruby scrambled around the bigger rocks and began to dig with her hands, hoisting the larger fragments aside with Hank's help. Sweat beaded on her forehead and her torn fingernails stung.

Heather gasped. "Movement."

With an explosion of rock and dust, Cooper sat up, coughing and caked with dirt.

Ruby hastened to him, grabbing his hand and wiping the grime from his face with her sleeve while Hank and Heather worked on freeing his legs. Desperately she tried to convince herself that Cooper really had just risen from underneath pounds of rubble, living, breathing and coughing.

Tears spilled from her eyes, and she dashed them away. "Are you all right?"

He groaned. "Now I know how a grape feels when it's juiced."

She squeezed his fingers, holding in hysterical laughter, reassuring herself that she was not imagining his reappearance. "Seriously, can you move your legs?"

"Yes, he can," Heather said, rubbing her shoulder. "He just kicked me."

"Sorry," Cooper said, blinking. "Reflex. What are you two doing here?"

"Let's get you out of this junk pile, before we have that conversation. I'm not sure about the stability of the situation at the moment." Hank cleared away the last heavy rock. "Can you stand?"

Cooper did, with Ruby holding on to one arm and Heather supporting the other. Slowly they clambered away from the fall and farther up the path where they found a place to rest. Ruby helped Cooper ease down on an exposed root. His arms and legs were scraped raw, and a trickle of blood snaked a muddy path down his forehead.

Cooper took her hand. "I couldn't hear a thing under that pile. I was worried about you."

She shook her head. "You were worried about me? You're the one that got pancaked."

"Juiced, I believe, is the metaphor we're going with."

He was so completely ridiculous, talking of metaphors and worrying about her, his eyes and teeth stark white against the grime of his face. She hugged him close and squeezed him. The thud of the pulse in his throat beat strong against her cheek. She pulled away, shaky. "Sure you're not hurt?"

He let out a breath. "I was just going to ask you that."

Heather perched on a rock next to him. "All right. I think we've established that neither one of you are seriously injured so let's move on. Confession time. I heard that you were headed to the lake to poke around. It piqued my interest, and I thought I'd follow in case you found anything noteworthy. Dad refused to let me go hiking alone, so he came with me. My phone fell out of my pocket somewhere along the way so Dad and I split up to try and find it. While I was crawling around, I heard the mountain come loose."

"Where'd you happen to hear about our plans?" Cooper shook his head. "Ah, let me guess. From Peter. I forgot, you're buddies."

Heather shrugged. "Good thing he mentioned it. We parked on the main road, and Dad and I saw you take this path so we hiked after you. Got here just in time to see the rocks come down."

Hank lifted an eyebrow. "What exactly are you looking for at the lake? I didn't get the particulars from Peter."

Cooper shot Ruby a look. There was no way she wanted to tell a reporter about her wild theory regarding the fish that swallowed the locket.

"We're the outdoorsy types," Cooper broke in, gingerly moving his arms and legs. "Don't need a reason to hike, do we?"

"I don't believe you're out here for fun," Heather said.

"Neither do I," came a deep voice. Sheriff Pickford eased his way over to them, wearing civilian clothes.

Ruby stared.

He took in her surprise. "Was out on my dock. Heard the rockfall and a scream. Boated over."

"After you heard the scream?" Cooper repeated.

"Yeah. That's what I said."

Ruby caught Cooper's eye, but they kept quiet about the engine noise they'd heard before they'd started the disastrous exploration and Pickford made no mention of the angry scene they'd witnessed between him and Molly.

"A nosey reporter and two careless hikers," Pickford said, ignoring Hank's presence. "Typical. Do I need to get a rescue crew here, or can you manage to get off this cliff by yourself? I can take one of you at a time in my boat, if you need it."

Cooper straightened. "I'm fine. Just a little banged up."

"Uh-huh." Pickford shook his head. "So if your memory isn't too muddled, why don't you tell me why you're really hiking here, since Miss Bradford and her sidekick already opened up that can of worms?"

Cooper opened his mouth to answer, but Pickford held up a beefy hand. "Don't bother lying, kid. I've been lied to by the best."

Ruby thought Pickford's eyes flickered to Hank for a fraction of a second.

Cooper cleared his throat. "Okay. We saw a cave, partially covered over by foliage. There." He pointed. "Figured it was worth exploring."

"To see if there was something we missed in our investigation all those years ago?" Pickford's eyes narrowed.

"To see if there was anything we could find to help," Ruby insisted. "We're not looking to blame anyone."

"It's been twenty years," Pickford said, eyes on the cave. "Why look here? Why now?"

Ruby swallowed. "I believe someone threw Alice's locket in the lake." She told the rest of her theory.

Heather's eyes popped and she patted her pockets for a pencil. "This is incredible."

"And none of it's going in the paper," Pickford growled.

Heather didn't answer.

"Ruby's theory may be just that, a theory," Hank said. "There will have to be some proof found that whoever took Alice came here." He frowned. "And will it do any good? That's the big question. Will it change anything at all?"

Cooper stood up, shaking more debris from his hair. "It's worth a try," he said. "I'm going into that cave."

"Uh-uh," Pickford said. "If anyone's going in there it's me. I'll get some ropes, call in a crew, we'll do it properly, even though I'm sure it's a waste of time and resources."

"No offense, Sheriff," Cooper said. "But another rockfall can seal off that place for good or bury any evidence too deep to recover it. I'm light and agile and I've already been buried once today, so I'm going to mosey on over to that cave and take a peek."

Pickford squared his shoulders. "And if I don't let you?"

"Well, I suppose you could arrest me, but I don't see on what grounds. This is private property and I'm invited, aren't I, Ruby?" He beamed at Ruby and she felt herself blush at his roguish grin.

"And I'm pretty sure I'm the only one who was invited to this shindig." Cooper's gaze raked the group.

An admiring smile played across Hank's face. "Well played."

Pickford's eyes flashed with venom. "You stay out of this."

Hank's smile dimmed. "You can't bully anyone here," he said quietly.

Pickford locked eyes on Hank and Heather stepped between them. "What's it going to hurt, Sheriff? There are people to summon help if Cooper gets into trouble. Seems like most of the slide debris has already passed. Five minutes, and it's done."

"Ten." Cooper grimaced. "I'm not at the peak of my game."

"Ten," she corrected with a smile. "What can ten minutes hurt after twenty years of wondering?"

Cooper didn't wait for an answer. He snaked an arm around Ruby's shoulders and bent close. "You sure you're okay with this?"

She put her mouth to his ear. "Yes, but before the slide, I thought I heard a scraping noise, as if…"

"Someone pushed those rocks down on us," he finished. "I thought the same thing. And now here we have Hank, Heather and Pickford on the spot. Odd, huh?"

She shivered. "Yes, odd."

"Stay close, and if anything looks like trouble, get out of the way. Promise?"

"Oh, I'll be close all right."

A worried look crept into his eyes. "Because you're coming with me into that cave, aren't you?"

"Yes," she said. "Someone has to keep you from being juiced again."

He sighed, the playful smile gone. "Ruby, I have a bad feeling about this."

In truth, she did, as well. Something about the shadowed entrance chilled her inside. "We have to know."

"Are you sure you want to?"

"Like you said, Cooper, the cave may not give us the answer we want, but it might be the answer we need."

He cocked his head, and pressed a kiss to her temple. "You are a brave woman, Ruby."

She repeated the words over in her mind, wishing she could convince herself as they inched toward the dusky access to the cave.

Cooper felt Ruby's hand grow cold in his. It was not the fact that the rock face above them blotted the sunlight, he knew, and he wasn't immune himself to the uneasy feeling. The dank air wafting from the entrance made the back of his neck prickle. As they approached, one careful footstep at a time, he heard the others fall in behind them.

His body ached, ribs feeling like they did when he'd played college football, the various scrapes and abrasions stinging with every small movement. The pain was not something he'd admit to Ruby, or anyone else. He moved ahead of her a pace as they drew closer to the entrance, which was a wide crack in the rock some three feet across. The cave was far enough away from the slide that it was still relatively clear, except for some debris that had collected at the mouth. A fringe of moss clung to the sheer periphery, trailing over the rock like a woman's wind-tossed hair.

Pickford was now nearly treading on Ruby's heels, and she shot him an annoyed look. "We've got to go one at a time here," she snapped. "The path is narrow."

"If there is anything to find, police should be first in," Pickford said.

Cooper didn't bother to answer. He let go of Ruby's hand and edged along before Pickford could push his way forward. A web of roots hung down in the gap, dead remnants of a massive tree, probably a fir, by the looks of it, that had been toppled in a rock slide or struck by lightning. The twisted coils hung in a silvered tapestry, level with Cooper's waist. No wonder the cave had been hard for any searchers to find.

He bent to crawl under the roots, a hollow snap echoing from under his foot. He peered down. Bone. Something shot out of the mass of roots. Cooper jerked back into Ruby. Heather screamed as the thing careened by them.

"Saw-whet owl," Ruby panted after a moment. "Nocturnal. We woke him up."

Heather laughed. "He woke me up, too."

Ruby pointed up in a tree where the little bird

with the oversize head had come to rest, glaring at them with yellow eyes. "They don't like visitors, and they're excellent hunters."

"That explains the bones." Cooper pointed to the remnants of a rodent skull. Ducking low and ignoring the protest from his ribs, Cooper managed to creep under the roots and squeeze inside.

Cold stone walls chilled his shoulders. The sunlight penetrated only the first foot or so of the cave, leaving the rest in blackness. He took his phone out of his pocket and activated the flashlight app. At least that still worked, regardless of the thick walls and the fact that it had nearly been crushed by a rock slide not an hour ago. Tiny flecks of crystals danced and sparked in the light. Lessons from a long-ago geology lecture kicked in as he noted the walls were basalt, which explained why the cave was still there. Pure sandstone would have worn away over time. Stripes of fawn-colored stone twined together with darker pockets. He wished he could see it in the daylight. The colors were probably incredible.

The floor of the cave was covered with rocks of all sizes, some worn smooth and others jagged. He hoped they would not disturb any other wildlife. He felt Ruby's hand on the small of his back.

"Any chance we're going to upset a bunch of bats?" he whispered.

"It's possible, but an owl isn't usually going to roost in the flight path of a bat colony."

"Good. I've been in a bat exodus before and it's not pretty. There was plenty of noise and not all of it from the bats." The cave was oblong in shape, no more than ten feet deep and six feet high. He could not stand straight without the risk of smashing his head on the rocks above. Pickford managed to cram into the space in spite of his bigger frame, waving a small flashlight around.

"Looks like part of the ceiling came down a while back." He played the light over the rock surfaces. "Not much here but a mess."

Cooper felt the twin pangs of relief and disappointment. "Like I said, it was just a whim. I'll sleep better knowing we checked it out."

Ruby sighed, a small sound oddly amplified by the cave. "A whim," she repeated. "Maybe finding the locket will amount to nothing. More unanswered questions."

Pickford raised his hand as if to pat her on the shoulder but lowered it again without touching her. "It can make you crazy if you let it, honey," he said, softly. "Happens way too often in my line of work. More questions than answers."

Heather and Hank squirmed inside behind them.

Pickford huffed. "I told you two to stay out."

"You aren't my boss, Sheriff Pickford." Heather smiled at him. "And I don't have to do what you say in this case."

Pickford's chin went up. "Self-serving. So like your father."

Hank stepped nearer. "Let's not go there, Sheriff. Not now."

"Why not? Been waiting to have a conversation since you started sniffing around town, but you haven't been at the diner when I've come to call."

Hank smiled. "I guess you've visited at the wrong times." He paused. "It's been nice catching up with Molly, though."

Heather grabbed her father's arm. "Dad."

Pickford might possibly have taken a swing at Hank with his fisted hand if Ruby hadn't cried out at that moment.

They all stopped and stared at her.

Cooper crunched across the floor. "What? What is it?"

Her hands were pressed to her mouth, so he followed her gaze to the floor. His heart sank as he saw the white gleam shining in the rubble, the perfect, graceful shard of a human skull.

NINE

Horror swirled up through Ruby's stomach, engulfing her mind and heart in a numb cloud. She heard Pickford ordering them all from the cave, saw Cooper's shoulders droop as he followed Heather and Hank outside. Heather protested, but Pickford stood firm.

"Now, it is a possible crime scene, and you'll do what I tell you or I'll arrest you right here." He took out his phone and, finding a signal, called for help.

Hank stood next to his daughter, a hand on her shoulder, a look of shock on his face.

Heather shook her head. "I can't believe after all these years, Alice has finally been found."

After all these years, Ruby's mind echoed.

"We don't know that for sure." Cooper stood close, peering into Ruby's face. "Are you okay?"

Okay? She felt in that moment she would never be okay again. Alice, little Alice, once a living breathing child, was now a brittle skeleton discarded on an unforgiving floor of stones. It could just as easily have been herself lying there. He pulled her to him, pressing her shivering body close to his. She could not feel it or anything else.

"Try to tell me what you're thinking," he murmured into her ear. "Can you? Put words to the feelings?"

His voice seemed to come from someplace far away. She forced her mouth into motion. "I'm thinking about Josephine and Lester. All the time searching and wondering. How will they feel knowing she was here the whole time not three miles away? That they might have been so close to saving her but instead she…" Dizziness overtook her and he eased her down onto a rock, kneeling before her, stroking her shoulders. "I hope she didn't suffer."

"She's not suffering now. Hang on to that." His eyes were tender, filled with the same sorrow as she imagined her own were. He wiped tears from her face that she hadn't known were falling. "We don't know anything yet, for sure. Let's try to take it one step at a time."

"Oh, Alice." She closed her eyes and when she opened them again, Hank and Heather had drawn close. Hank sat nearby, face strained, elbows propped on his knees as Heather typed notes into her phone.

Cooper glared at Heather. "Please say you're not writing this up."

"Notes, is all. Not an article. Not yet."

"Yet? If this is Alice, a family's life is ruined."

Heather eyed him steadily. "It was ruined twenty years ago, Cooper. This is just the last chapter. The Walkers deserve to know. And so does your family. So does Peter."

"We shouldn't be here." Hank rubbed a hand over his face. He had been handsome once, Ruby knew, but now weariness sagged his features and his eyes were dull and hopeless. "Makes things harder for Pickford."

"He doesn't like you, does he?" Cooper sat next to Ruby, arm tightly around her. "What's his beef?"

Heather snorted. "Thinks he owns the town. He's a bully at heart."

"He believes he had good reasons for hating me," Hank said.

Ruby frowned. "What reasons?"

Hank raised an eyebrow. "You really don't know?"

Ruby's mind simply would not cooperate. She shook her head. "My father said there was bad blood between you, but he never told me why."

Hank laughed softly. "Not surprised that you'd be in the dark. Perry is happy to wallow in the mud to accomplish his ends, but he would never track any home in case it might soil his own family."

"What is that supposed to mean?"

Heather looked up from her phone. "Your father ruined mine, didn't you know that? They really do keep you in the dark."

Hank held up his hand. "It's not the time to go into it."

"What better time?" Heather said.

"Heather…" Hank warned.

She waved him off. "Perry Hudson proved, or thinks he did, that my father was a thief."

Ruby was about to answer when Pickford emerged. "Team's on its way up. You four are staying here until we get individual statements."

What followed was a grueling hour. They were escorted along the trail back to a spot near the lake where they answered questions and waited to be taken back to the sheriff's office for yet more questions. She told them every detail again and again, including her suspicion that the rock slide had not been a natural occurrence. The officer she spoke to did not comment, but she could read the doubt on his face easily enough.

A medic checked Cooper over and found no serious injuries to speak of. She was given a musty-smelling blanket to wrap around her, to ward off shock, she knew. It didn't even come close. Facts kept whizzing through her mind in a blur. Alice. The cave. Heather's accusation against her father. And strangest of all, the accidental rock slide that may not have been an accident.

Was it possible that someone wanted Cooper and Ruby to die on that windswept slope? The thoughts jounced and banged through her mind as she and Cooper, with their law enforcement escorts, were loaded into a sheriff's car and driven back to Ruby's house.

Her father was loading dead branches into a trailer when he saw the vehicle approach. His mouth went slack, his body rigid. She hastened from the car, anxious to rid him of the fear that she saw played out on his posture.

Wrapped tight in his hug, she whispered, "It's okay. We're okay. They found her." She could manage nothing else as the tears choked her throat and poured down her face. Her father spoke to the police for a moment and led Ruby inside. When she was sitting on the worn sofa that had always been more suited for a San Francisco Victorian than an Oregon cabin, her father pressed a mug of hot tea into her hand. Ruby didn't like tea, but she knew it made her father feel better to tend to her in this way, so she sipped dutifully. Cooper seemed to relish his mug of Earl Grey.

"Foolish, you know." Perry looked at both of them as he spoke. "You could have been killed, hiking up there alone. Isn't that what your brother always says?"

Mick spoke from the doorway where he'd been listening. "That's word-for-word what I say." He shot a look at Cooper. "It was your idea? You talked her into it?"

Cooper raised an eyebrow. "In case you haven't noticed, your sister has a mind of her own."

Mick allowed a rueful smile. "Yeah. I noticed." He rubbed the back of his neck with his palm. "Talked to a cop as he was leaving. They found Alice's body?"

Ruby swallowed hard. "It looks that way."

Mick sighed. "Now they can solve it. Finally."

The room lapsed into silence, and Ruby became aware that Mick and Cooper were staring at each other.

Cooper put down his mug. "Gonna say it, Mick?"

Mick stood, fingers tucked in the waistband of his jeans. "Glad it's going to be over. Josephine deserves justice."

"Yes. Peter does, too."

"Well," Mick said softly. "I guess we're about to see how that all works out."

"I guess we are." Cooper's eyes grew so cold that Ruby could not stand it. She looked away wondering if their grisly discovery in the cave would bring long-awaited peace, or more destruction.

Cooper fought against the rage that coursed through him, unexpected and strong. Every time he thought he'd won over the anger, it came through potent as ever. He'd prayed about it every night of his life and there was still no permanent relief. He took in the family in the kitchen, allied, thick as a family could be.

Remember, Cooper. They will be thrilled to see Peter demolished. He shot a look at Ruby who stared at her shoes. Even her? Would she delight in the annihilation of his brother if it meant saving her own family? The thought burned for some reason. But Peter was innocent. Innocent.

"There will be physical evidence in that cave," Mick said. "There has to be. Enough to convict."

"Or exonerate," Cooper added.

"Look, Cooper. I know you want your brother to be in the clear. I get that. But I'm a former parole officer, and I'm naturally a suspicious guy and Peter never could produce anyone to give him an alibi. All these years and nobody could prove he wasn't the guy Ruby saw in the woods."

"Even if Peter was there, right there, just before Alice was taken, it doesn't make him guilty. As a former parole officer, you must have read people wrong sometimes, didn't you?"

The arrow hit its mark. Knowing he should feel ashamed of throwing Mick's past failure back at him didn't stop him from doing just that. Mick flinched, and Cooper turned to Perry. "We've run into two people today who aren't your biggest fans."

Perry sat stiff backed, hands on his knees. "Oh?"

"Stumbled upon an argument between Molly and

Sheriff Pickford on the main road. Gonna tell us why Pickford hates you?"

"Does he have to?" Mick fired off. "It's not your business."

"Ah. A Hudson family secret?"

Perry's lips tightened ever so slightly. "No. No secret. If you want to know, I'll tell you. Sheriff Pickford has trouble with the 'don't shoot the messenger' philosophy. Twenty years ago, I was hired by Jeff Ringer, the owner of Spruce Lodge, to find out who was skimming from the restaurant profits. I did some routine work, photographing and such. I was able to prove it was Hank."

"Hank Bradford?" Ruby gaped. "He was stealing?"

Cooper knew there was more. "And you found out something else, didn't you? In the course of your investigation?"

Perry's gaze traveled around the room before he answered. "I learned that Molly Pickford was involved with Hank."

"Having an affair, you mean," Cooper said.

"Yes. It changed Wallace, to find that out. I think he could forgive the infidelity in time, but the way he found out was painful."

"You didn't tell him, Dad?"

He sighed. "I knew Molly. She'd always been a good friend, helped me get settled in here, and you know how she's been a mother figure to you, Bee."

Ruby nodded.

"Anyway, Molly begged me not to tell Wallace right away. She wanted a few days to figure out how to break it to him, so I complied. I provided him with evidence about Hank's stealing, but I kept quiet about the affair until Molly could tell him. He felt… unmanned, I think when he did find out."

Cooper grimaced. "I can see how he would feel that way."

"Particularly because he didn't hear it first from her. Small towns have robust gossip mills. Someone figured it out and everyone in town got wind of the affair before Molly could tell her husband. Pickford blamed me, accused me of hiding the truth and never intending to tell him. Wallace's paranoia has just gotten worse over the years and he will never believe that Molly and I are just friends, nothing more."

"I didn't think about it before, but I remember the sheriff driving by our house sometimes, when Molly was visiting," Ruby said.

"And now Hank has been popping into town again with Heather, helping her with her story." Cooper folded his arms. "That's got to make Pickford a little nuts, but the argument we saw was about you, Mr. Hudson. I'd say Pickford is not comfortable with the fondness between you and his wife."

Mick stood. "Cooper, my dad and Molly are friends. That's all. Don't imply anything else."

Cooper put down his mug and got to his feet. "I'm not implying. Pickford was. I'm just telling you that you've got enemies in this town, too. Some people consider the Hudsons to be the bad guys." Cooper headed for the door, catching himself before he spewed out something to further fan the flames. *What was he doing?* He contemplated that as he stepped into the dappled sunlight. Trying to get even somehow? For what? The Hudsons thought the same thing everyone else did in the town. And why did his anger feel a whole lot like fear?

He finally realized that someone was calling his name. He turned as Ruby caught up with him.

"Cooper…"

Her eyes were moist, cheeks flushed with two blooms of color. He swallowed. "Yes?"

"That got out of hand." She blew out a breath. "I just came out here to thank you for believing in my idiotic theory about the fish."

He felt the anger ebb several notches. Why could he not sustain a nice head of steam when she was around? "Maybe not so idiotic. It did lead us to the cave."

She shuddered. "Yes, and nearly got you killed."

"I'm fine. We'll know more in the next few days." He wished he could recapture the same light, ebullient feeling he'd shared with Ruby not three hours before, when they'd hiked through the magnificent forest, the place where both their passions entwined.

"I'm going to take a shower, then, go into town and talk to Peter. Make sure he's aware."

"May I... Could I catch a ride with you?"

He blinked in surprise. "Sure. Why?"

"My dad's going to need the truck, and I wanted to bring Josephine some flowers."

He saw the sadness there on her face, and it cracked a piece of his heart. All his anger melted away, and he took her hand. "They won't tell her anything, I'm sure, until they're certain and the doctors feel she can handle it physically."

"I know. I was remembering that Alice was looking for flowers, the day she was taken." Ruby turned anguished eyes on him. "She was going to bring them to her mother."

Cooper gathered Ruby to his chest then and held her steady against the tide of grief that washed through them both. Then his lips found their way to hers.

An electric spark warmed his mouth, trickling into his heart and jumping along each nerve in turn. He slid his palm around her head, urging her closer, melding the two of them into one.

When he let her go, they stood for a moment, breathless.

Why had he given himself permission to kiss her like that?

And why had that kiss turned his heart upside down?

TEN

Ruby sat in a patch of sunlight outside Cooper's cabin while he showered, and mulled over the kiss. Her heart still thudded as she savored the feeling of his lips on hers, but the task that lay ahead cast a pall over the warmth. She dreaded the thought of seeing Josephine, but she knew it was her duty. They didn't speak much during the drive to town. What was there to say?

She could not imagine how the bizarre situation could be contained in words. The town of Pine Cliffs boasted more amenities than its tinier counterpart of Silver Peak. It was a place she'd only visited a few times. She had the same disconnected feeling she always did when she found herself in a place with many people, the disorientation she imagined a bear might feel as it emerged from hibernation. The Hudson family really had created a place apart, away from the hustle and bustle, removed from the community. Something uneasy floated up her spine, a vague and unsettled flutter.

Heather's words came back to her. *They really do keep you in the dark.* No, her dad was protective, that was all.

They parked at The Evergreen, an old, rustic-style diner. At a little after two in the afternoon, the place was less than half-full. The smell of food made Ruby's mouth water, reminding her she hadn't eaten since the night before.

"Buy you lunch?"

Ruby laughed. "Can you hear my stomach growling?"

"Not over the sound of my own." He led the way in and they perused the handwritten chalkboard menu, which as Hank said, changed daily. The current offerings were a sundried tomato, basil and ham sandwich and spicy tortilla soup.

"My dad would be excited about the soup. He thinks soup is nature's perfect food. He always starts by putting a hunk of bread in the bottom of the bowl before he ladles up the soup. Mick does the same thing."

"Tempting idea. Two of the specials," Cooper told the teen waitress.

"And a cup of coffee," Ruby added as they slid into a booth. The teen filled a mug for her and told them she'd bring the rest of their order shortly.

The waitress told them Peter would be on a break soon.

Ruby cupped the mug, holding it under her chin. "I can't seem to warm up."

Cooper nodded, distracted. She was sure his mind was still on the scenario just played out with her family, or perhaps it lingered where hers did, in the quiet cave, halfway up the sandstone cliffs. Or could he possibly be remembering, and regretting, the kiss?

Molly Pickford plopped onto the booth seat next to Ruby, enveloping her in a hug that nearly spilled her coffee. Ruby returned the embrace. "I'm so glad to see you." She clung to the woman for a moment, holding tight to the comfort, allowing Molly to kiss her cheek. Molly was in her mid-fifties, with sparkling brown eyes and a chic bob of hair. Her vivacious personality was not a match for Wallace's, for sure, Ruby thought.

"I stopped by to see you a half hour ago, but Perry said you'd headed into town." She smiled at Cooper and introduced herself. "You must be Cooper Stokes. We've never officially met. I heard you were back in town, visiting your brother."

Cooper sighed. "News travels around these parts."

"You have no idea."

Ruby tried to get Molly to join them for lunch, but the woman declined. "Listen," she went on, eyes wide. "Perry said you found a locket, and Josephine went after you with a knife and her husband attacked you also." She squeezed Ruby's shoulders.

"Are you okay? Perry insisted you were, but I had to see for myself."

So much had happened in the past few hours, she'd almost forgotten the locket. "I'm okay, thanks to Cooper."

Molly beamed another smile at him. "Knight in shining armor?"

"No. Botanist in the right place at the right time."

"I see. Modest, too." Her smile dimmed. "There's something going on. Wallace has been at work since this morning and was supposed to be off at noon. He doesn't fill me in, of course."

Ruby looked down at her coffee.

Molly nodded. "You know what it is, don't you?" She waved a hand. "Don't worry. I won't press you. I'll wait to find out with the masses."

"I'm sorry," Ruby said.

"Don't be, sweetie." She pressed a kiss to Ruby's cheek. "You're one of the few people I know who doesn't have something to be sorry for." She got up.

Cooper stood when she rose to go, earning another bright smile. "He's a keeper," she said.

Ruby flushed. "We're not…"

Cooper interrupted. "You said Wallace has been at work all day?"

She nodded. "I saw him long enough to have an argument with him this morning, but that's it." Her eyes narrowed. "Why do you ask?"

"I'm a nosey botanist."

"Oh, I think there's more to you than that." She gave him a slow smile, then her gaze drifted to the counter. Ruby wondered if she was looking for Hank. "Anyway, I've got to go. Can't stay around here long or I'll find myself the subject of that rumor mill." She wiggled her fingers at Ruby and left.

Cooper sat again and the waitress delivered their lunches. Ruby toyed with her spoon. "Why did you ask about Wallace?"

"Because she said he'd been on duty all day, but when he arrived at the lake, he was wearing civilian clothes."

"So he must have changed."

"Funny, huh?" Cooper said.

Ruby didn't answer. Funny was not the word she would have used.

They did not see Peter during their meal so Cooper asked the waitress when he paid the bill. "He's been on dish duty since the breakfast shift. I think he's taking a break out back, right now."

Cooper thanked her and they exited the diner, circling around the back to a small break area for the employees. Peter was seated at a sun-worn picnic table with Heather Bradford. Unaware of their approach, Ruby saw him lean over and kiss Heather on the mouth. She returned the kiss, caressing his cheek.

Cooper slowed, stiffened. "I didn't realize they were that close."

Neither had Ruby. Heather popped the caps off the two glass bottles on the table in front of her and offered one to Peter. They clinked bottles and both drank deeply. Ruby heard Cooper's sharp intake of breath, felt his body stiffen next to her. He bolted toward them.

"What are you doing?" he demanded.

Peter and Heather jerked in his direction.

"Hey, little brother. What's up?"

Cooper grabbed the bottle from his brother's hand. Ruby was just close enough to read the label.

"If you wanted a root beer," Peter said quietly, "you could've just asked."

Ruby could feel the wave of embarrassment emanating from Cooper as he slid the bottle back onto the table. "I'm sorry. I thought it was something else."

"I know what you thought." Peter cocked his head. "Heather is aware that I'm an alcoholic, and she isn't going to tempt me to break my sobriety."

Heather gave him a disdainful look. "Whether you believe me or not, I care about your brother. I'm not using him and I'm not going to hurt him." She got up. "Why don't you two chat? I'll give you some space." Peter protested, but Heather waved him off and went to sit in a plastic chair a few yards away, sipping her root beer.

Ruby also stepped away as Cooper sank down next to his brother. Cooper's shoulders slumped, head bowed. Ruby's heart squeezed. He had leaped to the wrong conclusion and shamed his brother in front of Heather. Could the situation be any more painful?

Heather gulped some root beer. "Cooper should have faith in Peter."

Ruby bridled. "Easy for you to say. You don't know what he's been through."

"And you do?"

Heather's eyes bored into Ruby, and she realized she didn't really know what Cooper had endured, or Peter. Worse yet, until recently she hadn't really cared, thinking only about how Alice's disappearance had affected her own family.

She thought about Heather's prior revelation.

Your father ruined mine.

She'd been blind to so many things.

You didn't even realize what was going on right in your own household between your father and Sheriff Pickford, Hank and Molly. What else haven't you realized?

Heather shook her head. "Siblings. Makes me glad I don't have any."

"Only child?"

"Officially, I have a half sister. She's in the army serving in Germany. We're nothing alike, so I'm told." Heather tapped the empty bottle on her leg. "I suppose that's another pile of blame I could lay on your father, if I was inclined to be the whiney type."

"What?"

"My mother, Victoria, was pregnant when your dad proved my father was taking money and having an affair with Molly. Even though we moved away to some podunk town, my mother never got over it. They weren't officially married anyway, only engaged so I guess that made it easier for my mother to leave after I was a toddler. I stayed with my father and she moved on. Married a real-estate agent, had a daughter. Never showed much interest in me. It was as if she wanted to sponge away that portion of her life. And sponge me away in the process."

"Your dad made some bad choices. My father isn't to blame for that."

"Yeah, I guess," she added softly. "But you know what it's like to grow up without a mother, don't you? It's easier to blame someone else than accept the fact that your mother doesn't want you."

There was something stark and sad in Heather's eyes. Though Ruby wanted to think of Heather as her enemy, she found herself taking a seat next to her and letting the truth spill out. "I miss my mother, even though I never really knew her. That sounds weird. I have to know her through other people's recollections."

"Yeah. Been there. Still am. My father never wants to tell me a thing about Victoria, he's so ashamed of what he did stepping out on her, I guess." She watched Peter and Cooper talking. "Did you ever think that we're destined to pass on all our garbage to our kids?"

"What do you mean?"

"The infidelity thing. I've thought a lot about it. My dad's father cheated on his wife, and my dad in turn stepped out on my mother. Like it was in their genes or something."

Ruby looked for the glint of anger in Heather's eyes, but she did not see any. "You think Hank cheated because he learned it from his father?"

"Maybe. Only difference was my grandmother stayed in spite of her two-timing husband. My dad says she stuck it out in that marriage until she died of a heart attack. Never left that dismal airfield in Texas that they ran together even though he gave her plenty of reason."

"Do you think in the back of his mind Hank believed your mother would stick around, too, like his mother did?"

"I'm not sure. I think there were good reasons for my grandmother to stay in the marriage, which makes me wonder all the more."

"Wonder about what?"

"What kind of a woman could walk away from her child because of her husband's sins?"

The words fell quietly in the still space. Ruby thought about her own mother, desperately trying to dredge up memories that were not there. Did

Victoria not realize the pain of abandonment that Heather would feel all her life?

"You have no contact with your mother?"

"Ah, sure. Victoria sends me birthday and Christmas cards. Sometimes the odd gift arrives in the mail. She came to my high school graduation. I remember she wore a blue dress with matching heels."

How painfully small were those little tokens of love, and how deeply Heather must crave them. Maybe it was the same need that drove Ruby to try on her mother's elegant tailored clothing when she was sure her father was not around to see. To catch a scent of lingering perfume on the fabric, to see herself in the mirror and wonder if her hair was the same shade as her mother's, to try to feel something for a woman she had never known.

"That hurts."

"Yeah. I guess that's why I think so often of Josephine. I pried it out of my father after I read an article and began badgering him about it. First time I ever saw him cry. Josephine loved that kid, from what my dad says, doted on her." She laughed, a bitter sound. "A mom who doesn't want a kid, and one who would give her last breath to find hers. Ironic."

Ruby was thinking tragic was more like it. "It will be over for Josephine, soon." Her breath caught. "The wondering, I mean."

"And the hope, too." Heather stood. "I feel somewhat responsible for Josephine's pain. When I got permission from my publisher to investigate the story again, I looked her up. I asked a lot of questions about everyone, including you. Started her thinking and brooding, I'm afraid. Stirred the pot."

Ruby nodded. "Yes you did. She started wandering the woods, watching me."

"She won't get her daughter back, but there's one thing that she can still have and I'm going to keep digging until the truth comes out."

Ruby brushed off her jeans. "You're sure..." She stopped the question as it emerged.

"That Peter wasn't the one who snatched her?" She nodded, looking at him. "It wasn't Peter."

"How can you be certain?"

"I just am. My father's never believed Peter was guilty either. Peter's a good man, and he was destroyed by what happened. He's rebuilding his life now and I'm happy he's getting a second chance. When we find out all the pieces to the story, Peter is finally going to be able to stand up and show this town how wrong they were about him."

Ruby knew in Heather's mind the Hudsons topped the list of people who distrusted Peter. "My dad investigated and handed the facts over to the police. There was not enough evidence to charge Peter with a crime. We weren't out to get him."

"Yet he was still hanged in the court of public opinion." She jerked her chin. "Even you. For all your careful words and apparent open-mindedness, you believe he's guilty, deep down, don't you?"

Ruby found herself momentarily speechless. What did she think? Who should she believe?

Heather smiled. "That's what I thought. I'm going to go finish my lunch date with Peter before he has to go back to work." She paused. "You know Alice's abductor wasn't a stranger. It was someone in this town who everybody knows, maybe even respects. Someone living right out in the open as if they have nothing to hide."

Something cold slithered down Ruby's spine. "Who do you think it is then, if Peter is innocent?"

Heather shrugged. "That's what I'm going to find out."

Ruby watched her go, shoulders straight, chin thrust out.

Heather Bradford would not stop until the truth was revealed.

Every last bit of it.

ELEVEN

A half hour later Cooper drove them to a grocery store where Ruby purchased a dozen carnations. He took the road to the hospital, trying to fight off the heavy weight on his heart. He'd distrusted his brother. Again. Only this time Peter was on track, sober and doing all the right things.

"Do you want to talk about it?" Ruby offered in a soft voice.

"Not much to say." Fatigue weighed down every part of him, and his ribs throbbed a maddening tempo. "I can't seem to allow myself to believe in him, and I'm the one guy in the world who should."

"He's given you reasons to doubt."

"Yeah, he has. Once he had me convinced he was working a job in an airport café. Even had the uniform and everything."

"It wasn't the truth?"

"No. He got fired after two days, but he knew I'd kick him out of my place if I found out he'd been drinking again." He blew out a breath. "It hurts him that I expect him to fail, and I don't want to be that way, but the doubt always creeps back in."

She put a hand on his shoulder. He was grateful for the gesture and for the fact that she did not say anything. The touch was enough until she voiced the next question.

"When did he start drinking?"

Cooper slowed to allow a motorcycle to pass, an old Softail that reminded him of the banged-up model whose engine his brother had spent summers unsuccessfully trying to coax life back into.

"Flirted with it as a teen, after my dad died. Mom punished him, had Sheriff Pickford talk to him, all that. Seemed to scare him straight for a while. Then after Alice...well, his drinking got out of control."

"Could you trust him back then?"

It suddenly became clear where her mind had gone. Stupid he hadn't seen it sooner. He'd been too distracted by the comfort he gleaned from her physical presence. He pressed the accelerator. "Ruby, Peter lied about his drinking, not about what happened to Alice. He doesn't know. He didn't do it."

She looked away and it was as if he could hear her thoughts. How can you trust a liar? His reaction today behind the restaurant had shown him he didn't, not about the drinking. Did his love for Peter blind him to other lies? Bigger lies? *You know your brother, Coop. Ruby doesn't.* At least now he could understand where she was coming from. She had her own doubts and family secrets to contend with.

He breathed a prayer for wisdom to navigate the troubles he knew were just ahead and finished the drive faster than he should have.

Ten minutes later as they checked in at the lobby, he found himself asking in spite of the turmoil in his gut. "Do you want me to go with you to see Josephine?"

"No," she said, before blurting out, "yes." Her cheeks pinked. "Sorry. I'm not usually so flaky."

"No sweat. These are some strange times." Strange indeed, that he should somehow be happy about spending more time with Ruby, even under such harrowing circumstances. They rode up in the elevator, the pink blooms shaking in Ruby's hand. He marveled at her courage. As a kid he'd always thought courage was something heroes possessed, an absence of fear. He'd come to realize courage wasn't the absence of fear, it was acting anyway in spite of it, braving the hardships of this world knowing that there was a loving God in charge of it all.

What kind of courage did it take for this woman to face the unstable mother of her lost friend, knowing there would soon be no hope left to shelter Josephine from the terrible truth they'd found in the cave?

He held the door open and followed her in. Josephine was asleep, long silver hair fanned out

on the pillow. Ruby slid the flowers onto the bed-
side table next to another vase holding a trio of yellow roses. "Alice would have wanted you to have
these," she whispered.

Cooper squeezed Ruby's hand as Josephine's eyes
fluttered open.

"You came back," she croaked. "Come here
where I can see you."

Ruby bent over the bed. "Hello, Mrs. Walker.
How are you feeling?"

Josephine smiled. "Fine, just fine, baby. I've been
waiting for you for so long."

Ruby shot him a horrified look.

Cooper's stomach contorted. "Mrs. Walker, it's
Ruby Hudson and Cooper Stokes. We stopped by
to wish you a speedy recovery."

Josephine appeared not to hear, staring at Ruby.

"So glad you're here," she whispered. "So glad,
baby. I'm sorry for all the things I did. You forgive
me, don't you? Say you forgive me."

"Mrs. Walker." Ruby leaned closer. "I'm Ruby."

Josephine cocked her head, peering closely. She
reached up to finger a section of Ruby's hair. "Soft.
You brushed a hundred times like I taught you. It
shines in the light. Didn't I always say that, Alice?
One hundred times."

Ruby whispered. "I'm Ruby."

Josephine clutched Ruby's hand, kneading the

fingers in her own. "I was a good mother, most of the time. Good. Wasn't I?"

Ruby gasped. "Josephine, I'm so sorry, but I'm not Alice."

Josephine kissed Ruby's fingertips. "Never mind, honey. I left it in the hiding place, like I told him. You remember?"

"Him?" Ruby said.

"What did you leave, Mrs. Walker?"

"The locket. Your locket," Josephine whispered, bright eyes fixed on Ruby. "It's in the hiding place in the hollow. The one you showed me and Daddy. That's where I put the locket to keep it safe until Daddy comes back. I didn't want that girl taking it away from you again. Shouldn't be too long now."

Ruby stared at Cooper.

He reached in to free Ruby from Josephine's tight grasp as a nurse came in. "I've got to help Mrs. Walker tidy up. Would you mind stepping out?"

"We were leaving anyway," Cooper said. He pulled Ruby into the circle of his arm, felt her shivering against him, guiding her out the door into the quiet hallway.

"Come back soon, baby," Josephine called. "You've been away too long."

Ruby was breathing in little pants. "She thought I was Alice, and she thinks she's been talking to a man."

His own breathing was a little unsteady. "Lester hasn't shown up at the hospital. Maybe she's dreamed that she's been talking to him? Probably her medications. The confusion will clear up." Hollow words. How could knowing Alice's body had been found help Josephine face reality?

"Why did she keep saying she was sorry?"

He had no answer. "Do you know where this secret hiding place is she's talking about?"

Ruby closed her eyes in thought. "There was one place in the woods, the remnants of a mill where we used to play. Dad took us and let us poke around when he did surveys up there years ago. We pretended it was an old pirate ship and we found a place for our booty. It wasn't much of a secret hiding place, because I'm sure we told everyone about it. I think we even showed my Dad and Lester Walker one time." She gasped. "Could Josephine have put the locket there to keep it safe?"

"Let's go find out." They hastened to the elevator and Cooper stabbed the button. "Should we call Pickford?"

Ruby frowned. "I want to check it out ourselves first. He's got his hands full right now."

He certainly did. Soon Pickford was going to make his own visit to Josephine's hospital room and he would not be bringing flowers, just some news that would be the cruelest words a parent could ever hear.

* * *

In any other circumstance, Ruby would have hiked to the old mill, perhaps made a day of it even, journaling about the birds she saw on the way. This time, she opted for the easier route. Rounding up some loppers and leather gloves, she placed them into the back of Cooper's double cab pickup.

"Why do I feel like Indiana Jones?" Cooper said with a smile.

"The sanctuary has no snakes or angry natives, that I know of."

"Except Lester Walker. He might turn up again."

She steeled her spine against a shiver. "If he does, I'm prepared this time." She patted the loppers.

Cooper laughed. "He could probably use a little pruning."

The easiness between them was a balm. What was there about Cooper that he was able to make her remember that she really did have a sense of humor buried down deep? Since she'd found the locket, there had been so little cause to smile, but Cooper found humor in the oddest of moments. Sunlight broke through the trees as he leaned against the car door, and he turned his face to it.

"That feels good."

She stopped and allowed the sun to warm her, too, accepting the gift that had been offered at that moment, sun in the midst of the storm that was brewing all around them.

Shoulder to shoulder with him, something rose inside her that felt like gratefulness—to Cooper for relishing the sunlight, and to God for sending the man to bring it to her attention. Gratefulness? It tickled at her insides along with the delicious warmth.

"How can you be peaceful? In the middle of all this?"

He sighed. "I'm not always. I've got plenty of defensiveness and a heap of anger, still. A friend of mine told me long ago when things with Peter were at their worst, that if you look for God, you find him in places you'd never expect." He waved a hand. "Like in some good old-fashioned sunshine."

Peace. What a light and lovely trail it left inside. "I haven't been looking. Not since Alice."

"I stopped looking for a while, too. Got lost in myself and my problems." He placed his arm around her shoulders. "He waits anyway while we stumble around."

For one precious instant, she allowed the idea to clatter through her soul. No matter how dark, He was there waiting.

Then she recalled the purpose of their mission.

To find proof to convict Alice's killer.

Alice, the girl who vanished when God hadn't lifted a finger to help.

She pulled away as her brother banged out of the house.

"Going somewhere?"

"To the old mill. We think Josephine may have hidden the locket there."

True to character, Mick did not ask unnecessary questions. "I'm going with you."

Ruby caught the expression on Cooper's face, halfway between amused and exasperated. Instead of arguing, Cooper made a show of opening the door with a sweeping gesture and a courtly bow. "My humble conveyance is at your disposal, Master Hudson."

Mick climbed into the back as Ruby took the front passenger seat. With Ruby's direction, Cooper drove them along the graveled road. At times they had to stop to clear away the dense shrubbery that had swallowed up the path.

"Not someplace you visit often?" Cooper said.

Ruby cleared her throat. "Not anymore."

Cooper took her hand, and she let him. Mick shifted in the backseat. With a sly glance in the rearview mirror, Cooper kissed her fingers.

The seat cushions complained as Mick continued to settle and resettle his big frame.

"Uncomfortable, Mick?" Cooper inquired, an innocent arch to his eyebrow.

"Keep your hands on the wheel. Get's treacherous in through here," Mick growled.

Ruby thought she saw a smile on Cooper's mouth as he grasped the wheel with both hands. Cooper may have matured into a man, but he retained a whiff of the mischievous boy he had been long ago. She remembered the kid with the scraped knees and dirty face who presented her with a single wild-flower and an invitation for a date. If things had been different...

Maybe they could be, her heart whispered. When the truth came out and Cooper's deepest desire was realized as his brother's name was cleared. Could the locket be the answer to the past and the key to a brighter future for all of them?

Cooper felt her looking and beamed a smile so dazzling it made her catch her breath. "Don't worry. I'm an excellent driver. Mario Andretti's got nothing on me."

She laughed. The engine growled up the slope, pinging rocks and loose gravel under the chassis.

Mick stiffened. "Did you hear that?"

Ruby peered around, seeing only the dense thicket that smothered the road on all sides. "What?"

"I thought..." He shook his head. "Must have been a rock hitting the car or something."

Cooper eyed him in the rearview mirror. "What exactly did you think it was?"

Their gazes locked. "Gunshot."

Cooper stopped the car and rolled down the windows. They listened for a long while.

"I don't hear anything," Ruby said, finally.

Mick nodded. "Could be I'm paranoid."

She understood. After fighting in a war as a marine, Mick lost his biggest battle at home as a parole officer whose misjudgment had cost a woman her life. The bitterness had raged inside her brother like a cataclysmic wildfire. "Do you want to listen for a while longer?"

"No. My mistake." Mick continued to stare out the window as Cooper drove on.

They reached a small hollow at the base of the windswept peak and piled out of the truck. Ruby tried to stop the memories from flooding back.

I brought some yarn so we can pretend to fish, Alice.

Will we catch anything?

Laughter filled the dusty space as two children transformed a ruined mill into a ship, heaving on the open ocean.

I think I hear the bad pirates coming, Bee. Should we hide?

No, we're safe. We're pirates, too. No one can hurt us.

"Oh, Alice," Ruby whispered. "Why did I not hear those bad pirates coming that day, twenty years ago?"

Mick strode toward something on the ground under the pine trees. He lifted the mass in his hands, feathers draping his palms.

She cried out and ran to him. That pile of white

and brown. It could not be. It must not be. "What happened?"

Her brother gently turned the little bird so she could examine it.

A kestrel, one of her kestrels, a female, lying broken and bleeding. The bird's eyes were opened, sightless, fixed forever on the sky from which it had plummeted. So small and fragile, it barely filled Mick's palms. She noted the wound through the bird's breast. Round, a bullet hole.

"Who would have done this?" she whispered, throat clogged with horror. "For what purpose?"

Cooper peered closer. "She's so small."

"Only four ounces or so," Ruby answered automatically, as if she was conducting one of the plethora of guided nature hikes. "About the weight of a candy bar." Her eyes traveled up to the nesting box, nailed to the top of a sturdy thirty-foot pole.

Mick shook his head, scanning. "Probably babies in there." He peered at the wood structure that their father had built over a decade before. "Something must have startled her. She flew out and…"

Another shot rang out.

TWELVE

Cooper dived into the shrubs, carrying Ruby with him. He managed to roll so he didn't crush her with his body and she came to rest on her side, staring at him with eyes so wide he could see his own shocked reflection.

Mick was on his stomach, peering out through the branches. "Came from up high, behind that peak of rock," he whispered. "I'm going to circle around."

"No, Mick," Ruby insisted. She tried to grab for him, but Cooper kept her pinned. She wriggled with all her might, but he held her tightly by the arms.

"Mick's a marine. He knows what he's doing."

"A former marine, and he needs my help. Let me go." Her thrashing did no good.

"There's no such thing as a former marine, I'm told. We're going to use a little common sense here and stay put." He sat up, keeping a firm grip on her forearm, peering through the bushes as he crouched.

She jerked to her knees. "You can't keep me here."

"Yep, I'm pretty sure I can."

Glaring, she yanked again. "You're a coward. We should be helping Mick."

"Name calling won't get you anywhere. I'm doing exactly what Mick would want, and you know it." He held fast.

"You can't do this." She gave a vicious yank.

Cooper only smiled, holding her as gently as he could. "Please, Ruby, stop pulling. I don't want to hurt you."

Anger clutched at her insides. "Cooper, stop it."

His mood shifted suddenly, and he pulled her to his chest. Her heart hammered at the serious twist of his lips, inches from her own. "Listen to me," he said, voice low and tense. "I'm bigger and stronger than you are. If you don't have enough sense to keep safe, I will keep you here against your will."

"Why?" she whispered, pulse roaring in her ears, the scent of whatever soap he used heady in her senses. "Why do you care what happens to me?"

He paused for a moment, the luscious depths of his eyes glimmering. "You're worth caring about." Then he kissed her hard and quick, enough to drive the breath out of her body before he pulled away.

She couldn't have run from him then if she'd wanted to. Her knees felt like gelatin and sparks of electricity shot through her body. There was no time to rally her senses as her brother jogged back into the clearing. Cooper rose and helped Ruby up. She wondered if he noticed the trembling in her fingers.

Mick fisted his hands on his hips. "He's gone. Or she. Didn't get a good look through the helmet."

Cooper stared. "Helmet?"

"Yeah. He was getting on an old motorcycle when I caught up."

"I noticed one on the way to the hospital. It could be a coincidence," Cooper mused.

Mick frowned. "In my experience, not much turns out to be coincidence in the end."

Ruby walked to the spot where Mick had laid the little kestrel. "But why shoot the bird? Why do that?"

"The intruder comes here to find the locket. Spooks the bird who flies out of the nest to defend her young." Cooper paused. "Does that sound right? Would a kestrel do that?"

"If they felt their nest was being threatened." Ruby could not take her eyes away from the poor bird. "But how did the guy know to come here? Why here? Why now?" The haunting conversation with Josephine came back to her. *I left it in the hiding place, like I told him.*

Ruby stared at Cooper. "Josephine told her visitor about the locket's hiding place, too."

"Think it could have been Lester? Maybe he's determined to have back what belonged to his daughter."

Mick grimaced. "I know he's got no regard for bird life."

"That's right. I remember when you got into an argument with Lester about the eagles." Ruby tried to recall the details.

"He was taking shots at our eagles. Looking to sell the feathers."

"I thought it was illegal to sell eagle feathers."

"It is, unless you've got a permit. Some Native American tribes are allowed, but the demand outstrips the supply. Feathers figure prominently in many ceremonial costumes." Mick frowned. "I went to see Lester years ago, before Alice disappeared, and told him if he ever took a shot at our eagles again, I'd turn him in and he'd do prison time and get fined."

"Things got ugly from there?"

"Yeah. We wound up in a fistfight."

"The night before Alice was taken," Ruby said softly.

"Which is why you were a suspect, too," Cooper said. "Before the suspicion shifted to my brother."

Ruby's stomach clenched as her sibling's face went dark. "He was cleared. Both my father and Molly vouched that Mick had driven to the edge of the property to clear a creek clogged up by the beavers."

Cooper remained silent, but Ruby could imagine his thoughts. A father and devoted family friend are not unbiased. Cooper and Mick stared at each other until Ruby could stand it no more.

"I'm going to see if the locket is inside. Are you two coming with me or not?"

Mick headed directly for the ruined entrance. Cooper followed without comment.

The air inside the dilapidated structure was cold, the light filtering through the broken stone walls cast flickering shadows like dark serpents over the floor. Scraps of iron and broken boards, spongy with rot, exuded a tang into the air. Try as she might, Ruby could not summon up the childish imagination she'd employed with Alice all those years ago. It was no longer a pirate ship, just a broken, forgotten place.

Alice, her heart cried out, remembering the little girl who had trusted her. Tears sprang into her eyes, and she froze, feet rooted to the cold floor.

"Bee?" Mick inquired. "Can't you remember where the hiding place is?"

"I remember," she whispered. Memories washed through her: innocent games, happy conversations, chocolate chip cookie snacks packed by Josephine Walker to be shared with Ruby. Then came fresher recollections: a lonely cave, the stark white of bones, the love that still shone in Josephine's eyes for a child who would never return.

Cooper moved close, placing his hand softly, ever so softly, on her shoulder. "You don't have to do this. Tell me where, and I'll find it. You can wait in the truck."

His voice was tender, as if he understood the anguish.

She swallowed hard. "No. Alice was my friend and I'm going to do what I can for her." Even if it's too late. She walked to the corner where a section of the wall stood strong against the elements. At the bottom was a little metal plate, the door of a small alcove set into the wall for some purpose she would never know. She pulled it aside. With fingers gone cold, she reached into the dark nook.

Cooper pushed forward, but Mick's wide shoulders blocked his view. He had to wait until Ruby stood up, brushing dirt off her jeans.

The defeat in her face told the story. Ruby wiped her forehead with the back of her hand. "It's empty. If the locket was there, it's not anymore. Maybe the shooter took it, or Josephine was confused."

"It's all right. We have more information to tell the Sheriff when they finish…" Cooper broke off, recalling the sad mission the police were currently enacting. "When they're available."

They trudged to the car and Mick began to paw through the piles of twisted metal that dotted the ground. "I'll find something to dig a hole with and bury the bird."

Ruby craned her neck. "Babies," she murmured. "This is the right time of year."

"Will the father be able to feed them on his own?"

"He'll have to work hard, especially if there's a big clutch, but it can be done. What I'm worried about are feathers. If the babies aren't old enough to keep themselves warm, they'll die of the cold while he's gone looking for food." She worried her lower lip between her teeth. "There may not be any babies at all, but if there are..." Her voice wobbled. "I can't stand the thought of them dying because their mother is gone."

The stricken look pierced Cooper's heart. "So I guess you need to know."

She shot him a look. "We'll go back to the house. Mick and I can drive up here again and we'll bring a ladder. We can probably do it by nightfall."

"I can save you a trip." Cooper walked to the pole holding the nesting box and began to shimmy up. Fortunately, he was still able to channel some of his eighth-grade PE skills. He was gratified to hear Ruby's gasp of surprise. The wood was rough, and he was glad the denim of his jeans protected his legs from splinters. Tiny shards of wood pierced his hands, no matter how carefully he grasped the old pole, but he wouldn't let her see him flinch. Sweat beaded his forehead as he climbed.

"I hear peeping," he called down.

"Be careful."

He kept going, one painful foot at a time. The discomfort would pass but if he could help keep this little bird family alive, it would somehow lighten the weight that Ruby was carrying around. The way she cared for the fragile creatures touched something inside him. He continued inching upward until he reached the hole and peered in. It was too dark to see, so he freed his cell phone from his back pocket and shone the light inside. Fuzzy heads on wobbly necks popped up to look back at him.

"I see two, no three babies." They began to wriggle and open their pale beaks wide. "Sorry, kiddos. I forgot to bring some worms along."

They started up some plaintive cheeping.

"Have they got feathers yet?" Ruby yelled up.

"Lots of gray fuzz and some patches of brown. What's your cell number?"

She laughed. "Odd time to be asking me for my number." She yelled it up anyway. He took a picture and texted it to her.

She scrutinized the photo. "They can stay warm. I'm so relieved."

He sighed. "Me, too." He'd been worrying about how to transport three baby kestrels down the pole without squashing them. "Okay, little fuzzy dudes. You take care of each other and wait for Papa. He'll have some grub for you."

Gingerly, he eased himself back down to the ground where Ruby squeezed him in a tight hug.

"Thank you. That was incredible, what you did."

He clutched her to him for a moment longer, wishing he could surprise her with another kiss.

Frankly the earlier kiss had been an impulse he hadn't seen coming and he knew he'd shocked her, but the memory of it stuck with him. The shock of being shot at?

Ruby took his hand and examined the palms. "Splinters. Sit down. I've got a first aid kit in the car."

He was going to tell her not to bother, but deep down he enjoyed the feel of her soft hand cradling his so he sat on a nearby stump until she joined him, grasping his fingers, armed with tweezers.

A frown of concentration creased her brow as she worked. The sunlight was waning, the rays dappling her hair with amber fire.

"Ouch," he said, flinching, as she applied a disinfectant wipe.

"Sorry. You're really good at climbing poles."

He grinned. "Like every other boy in America, I thought I wanted to be a firefighter. Seemed like learning about climbing would be a good place to start."

Her smile was perfect, breathtaking. "But you decided on botany instead?"

"I'd rather watch things grow up than burn down."

She bent over his hand again, and he could not resist caressing the luminous crown of her head with his free palm.

She tipped her face up, so his hand now cupped

her cheek. Her lips were parted, perfect, tempting him like the rarest flower in the forest. He moved closer, willing her mouth closer to his.

A loud clearing of the throat made Ruby jump to her feet. Her brother, Mick, held a shovel, broken at the top. "I've dug the hole. Do you want to bury the kestrel?"

The dark look on Mick's face made Cooper think the bird wasn't the only thing he'd like to bury. He remained seated while Ruby laid the little bird tenderly in the grave. All the while, Mick's eyes remained fastened on Cooper.

Mick was a dangerous man.

With a sister as beautiful as Ruby, he had good reason.

Cooper returned Mick's glare with a casual smile. *Deal with it, Mick.*

THIRTEEN

Cooper's chronic insomnia and thoughts of Ruby Hudson increased the deep fatigue that consumed him. He collapsed onto the lumpy mattress in the bedroom he'd claimed and didn't awaken until his internal body clock told him the sun had almost risen. He cracked an eyeball and tried to sort out the noises filtering through the cabin.

Rattling pipes indicated the shower was in operation. Peter, preparing to go to work. The rush of shame came back to him as he recalled the disastrous conclusion he'd jumped to the previous day. He'd apologized at the café. He felt the urge to do so a second time, to mend the damage he knew he'd inflicted.

Then anger won out again. *If you hadn't failed me so many times before, brother, I wouldn't distrust you now.* Anger, guilt, love and all the other emotions that came from living with an alcoholic bubbled together. Would he ever find peace? Only when Peter latched on to sobriety so tightly that it drove the doubt away. It was possible that day would never come. Through clenched teeth, he muttered the millionth prayer that his brother would have the strength. There was the murmur of conversation from the living room. Company?

His phone told him it was not yet six. In the same sweatpants and Smokey Bear shirt he'd slept in, he padded out to find Hank Bradford, talking in hushed tones on his cell phone. Hank's back was to Cooper.

"It wasn't my idea to come back here either," Hank snapped. "It won't be for long." He paused. "I know it makes you uncomfortable, but no one will find out. They'd better not." There was a note of menace in this last phrase as Cooper cleared his throat to announce his presence.

Hank whirled around, mouth open in surprise. He clicked off the phone. "Sorry. I didn't know you were there."

Cooper folded his arms. "Believe it or not, I live here, at least for a few weeks."

"Of course. Peter's car wouldn't start, so I came to give him a lift to work."

Cooper arched an eyebrow. "That's nice of you."

"Not really nice, more self-serving. He's our only dishwasher on duty for the breakfast service. Other one called in sick."

Cooper considered. Should he pretend like he hadn't overheard Hank's conversation? It would be the polite thing to do, but he was beyond being polite. Peter was heavily involved with the Bradfords, and Cooper wanted to know if they should be counted as friend or foe. "I'm sorry for intruding on your conversation. It sounds like you aren't altogether happy to be hanging out in Silver Peak again."

Hank was silent for a moment. "I'm not. Too many bad memories here, but I love my daughter and she's knee-deep in this Alice Walker investigation. I don't want her to get hurt and I'm here to make sure that doesn't happen. She's fond of Peter so I guess I'm taking him under my wing, too."

"And you don't want anyone to find out the truth." Cooper watched the flash of emotion flame up in Hank's eyes. "Sorry, but I heard that part, too."

"Good ears." Hank sighed. "I've done things I'm not proud of. Sometimes you can't just walk away from that."

Cooper played out his hunch. "Walk away from that...or walk away from her?"

Hank started. "How did you know I was talking to a woman?"

"Just a guess. Part of your old business was an affair with Molly Pickford, wasn't it?"

His eyes narrowed. "I shouldn't be surprised that it's common knowledge."

"Sheriff Pickford doesn't trust you around his wife."

"Sheriff doesn't trust anyone, but sometimes he's

right not to trust people." A shimmer in Hank's eyes, of guilt? Longing? Triumph?

"Are you and Molly involved again?"

Hank shoved his phone into his back pocket. "I don't think that's any of your business, now is it?"

Hank was right; it wasn't.

Peter came in, hair damp and cleanly shaven. "Sorry. Woke up late."

Hank nodded. "I'll wait for you in the car." He slammed the door behind him.

"Did you bother him?"

"Probably. I think he's having an affair with Molly Pickford again."

"Sheriff's wife? Nah. That's old news. He's involved with some other lady. Heard them talking on the phone a bunch of times and anyway, that isn't your business."

"You're not the first to say so, but Pickford and Hank are enemies. I don't want to have you caught up in that."

Peter straightened, a good inch taller than Cooper. "It's not your job to look out for me. Bad enough you embarrassed me in front of Heather."

"I apologized for that."

"Why do I get the feeling that I could cure cancer and negotiate world peace and you still wouldn't believe I had my life straightened out?"

Cooper's gut tightened. "I have reasons for distrust. So does Mom."

His brother slouched, shoulders slumped. "Yeah, I guess you do. This time I want to prove to you and Mom that I'm gonna make it but…"

"But what?"

He smiled, the textbook charming Peter grin. "Ah, nothing. Just got baggage is all. It's heavy."

"Always is."

Peter put Cooper in a good-natured headlock and rubbed his knuckles hard across Cooper's head until he pulled away.

"Gotta go, bro. There's a big pile of dishes with my name on it."

Cooper watched out the front door as Peter got into Hank's car and they drove away.

It was a glorious spring day, the sky clear of clouds except for a cluster in the distance in the direction of Sunstone Lake, which was now home to a crime scene. A chill clawed at his stomach as he closed the cabin door.

Ruby clicked off the phone, her mind boggled at her own boldness. What had spurred her to call Cooper and ask if he would like to hike with her up to the old mill to check on the baby kestrels? Mick would have gone, but for some reason she had not asked him. Perhaps she wanted to distract her mind from thinking about what the police had removed from the cave, and Cooper was just the person to do it. Maybe it was the light and easy feeling she'd gotten hiking with Cooper before, as if he understood her. The kiss rolled through her memory, once again bringing the heat to her cheeks.

"Feeling okay?" Perry looked up from his pencil sketch.

"Sure, yes. Just tired." She'd stayed up until nearly one o'clock explaining to her father everything that had transpired, after phoning the police station to tell them about the gunshots. "Going to town today?"

He nodded. "Meeting with the river preservation league." He paused. "Can you handle the three o'clock group?"

Ruby started. She'd nearly forgotten she was leading a sanctuary tour for a group of twelve birding enthusiasts. Excellent. Maybe it would get her mind off the insanity and back on track. She considered the crowning moment of the tour, the point where the group paused at the overlook to watch the eagles feed.

"Aside from the tour, I think it would be best for you to stay inside today while I'm out, until the sheriff can look into the shooting."

"We surprised whoever was going after the locket. I don't think it will happen again."

"Still…"

"I have to check on those baby birds, Dad. I'm not going to hole up here like a scared rabbit." She had the feeling she'd done too much of that already. "When do you think the police will be done in the cave?"

He heaved out a breath. "They're probably already done with the preliminaries. I imagine they will release a statement today."

Her breath caught. "After all these years. I can't believe it's really over."

He got up and embraced her tightly. "We're going to get through this, and then we can get back to normal."

Would there ever be a normal? "Dad, who do you think took Alice?"

He released her to arm's length. "The likeliest person is usually the one who did it."

Her breath grew short. "Peter?"

He didn't answer. "It's a bad idea for you to be around that family."

"But what if you're wrong?"

"The Stokeses represent the worst moment of your life. Do you really want that constant reminder?"

She took her father's hand, rough and calloused from the constant work outdoors, his cotton shirt stained by the oil paints he used to capture the glory of the Hudson Sanctuary raptors on canvas. "Pretending it didn't happen isn't going to work. I have to face it."

"And you think Cooper is going to help you do that?"

She blushed. How had he become aware of her attachment to Cooper? Was it that obvious? "He's just a good man. I didn't trust him at first, but I think I'm beginning to."

"Bee, blood is thicker than water and things are going to explode with the discovery of the body. Cooper will defend his brother even if it means causing you pain. Remember that."

She pulled away. "He wouldn't hurt me."

"He would, and what's more he'd do anything to save his kin."

"How do you know that, Dad?"

Her father seemed to age before her eyes. The light revealed patches of gray in his formerly dark hair, deep creases in his forehead. "Because Bee," he said softly, "I would do the same to save mine."

She did not know what to say to the man she'd thought she'd known so thoroughly. Now he seemed an enigma. "What are you thinking, Dad? Why do I get the feeling there's something you're not telling me?"

He stepped back and twirled the stub of a pencil between his fingers, looking out the window. "Your mother never liked the country. She was a city girl, all the way. After you two came along, I kept trying to convince her to move. We took a vacation here and I fell in love with the land, but she never did. Boy did we battle over it. Worst fights we ever had."

Ruby thought about the lovely dresses, the chic

clothes, the pictures of her mother's European travels before she met her husband. She smiled. "I can imagine."

"After she died, I packed up as soon as I could manage it, sold the house and bought this property." He looked toward the splendor of the sun lighting the latticework of branches. "I love it here, with every fiber of my being. Selfish of me, maybe, to have moved you here because it's where I wanted to be."

"Not selfish. We love it, too, Dad."

"But I know deep down it isn't what your mother wanted and sometimes…" He sighed. "I wonder if it was a mistake."

She wanted desperately to comfort him. "It wasn't."

He looked at her then, with eyes that saw down to the secret place. "You're a lot like her."

It was as if he knew she put on her mother's clothes sometimes, admiring the elegant garments in the mirror, and read the romance stories her mother had left behind about brave dukes and feisty governesses. Her cheeks heated up.

"She wanted other things for you, wanted you to go to church and learn about God."

Ruby knew it was a painful subject. "But we never did."

"I don't know how to give you your mother's faith, Bee. I never understood it." He let out a long protracted sigh. "I never understood what your mother saw in me, come to think of it, and I guess I don't understand what you see in Cooper."

She folded her arms and gave him a stern look. "There's no need to lecture me about Cooper. We're just friends, and he's only here another few weeks."

He fell silent, and she squirmed under the scrutiny, as if she was a little girl again, caught climbing trees in her best new school clothes.

"I brought us here, Bee." His voice was soft. "I let you go out on that day when Alice was taken. I... failed to protect you and Alice back then. I'm trying to do it now, to protect you and your brother."

Guilt, grief, fear twisted her father's face, and she could not bear it a single moment longer. She hugged him tightly and pressed a kiss to his cheek. "You can't protect me from everything, Dad."

"I've always known in my heart that what happened to Alice would rise up once more. I guess I've dreaded it, all these years, having it raked up again."

The rumble of an engine interrupted. "That's Cooper. We're going to check on the kestrels." She hoped her voice sounded firm and sure.

She and her father stepped onto the front porch as Cooper got out with a wave. They were in the middle of a strained round of small talk when another vehicle rolled up. The bottom fell out of Ruby's stomach.

Sheriff Pickford moved like a man who had not

slept in a very long time. His stubbled chin sagged, and his eyes were hollow and dull. "Sorry to intrude."

"No problem," Perry said. "Come in, you look like you could use some coffee."

"I would not say no to that," Pickford said, as they all followed Perry inside. Cooper took Ruby's hand and squeezed as they walked up the steps. She had not realized she was trembling.

"We'll get through it," Cooper whispered into her ear. "Together."

Together. She clung to the three syllables as they settled at the old Formica table where Alice and Ruby had sat so many years ago, coloring with their crayons and making paper chains.

Her father poured a steaming cup of coffee from the pot and placed it in front of the sheriff who inhaled deeply and took a swig. He pressed his hands around the ceramic. "Thank you."

Ruby couldn't contain the question. "What did you find out from the cave?"

Mick joined them, pouring himself a mug of coffee. "Didn't know you were here, Sheriff."

Pickford acknowledged him with a bob of his chin. "We've been working at the cave solidly since the discovery. There is a lot of debris so the best we can do is photograph and gradually clear the area without destroying any evidence. The body's been there for two decades, so it's unclear how much evidence we can glean from it at this point, but we're trying our best."

Perry nodded. "We know you are."

Pickford arched an eyebrow at him. "It's always cut at me that we didn't find her twenty years ago."

"We all failed that day," her father said quietly.

Ruby's vision blurred with tears. A sense of anguish built inside her that had started that day in the woods and leaped to flame again the moment she'd found the locket. She both dreaded and craved the announcement that Alice had been found, finally. Cooper held her tightly around the shoulders.

"Sheriff..." her voice broke and she could not ask.

He seemed to jerk back to the present. "I have to go soon and make a statement to the press after I visit Mrs. Walker in the hospital. Heather Bradford probably already knows everything since she's been parked just outside the crime-scene tape, eavesdropping. I think she's even tried to get in to see Josephine." He shook his head in disgust. "Reporters are vultures."

He rose. "Nothing is official yet, but I can tell you that the body found in the cave was not Alice Walker."

Ruby shot to her feet, knees wobbly. "What?"

Cooper gaped. "Who is it then?"

"We won't have an official ID for a while," the sheriff said, placing his mug carefully on the table.

"How about unofficial?" Mick asked.

"The skeleton is that of an adult male, and it's been there for two decades approximately. Unofficially," he swept the room with a calculating gaze, "I'd say we've found the body of Lester Walker."

FOURTEEN

Cooper's mind raced forward in a series of horrified starts and stops after the sheriff left. The body in the cave, which had lain there for years, was probably that of Lester Walker. It could not be. It was not possible. As they watched the sheriff's car rumble down the gravel road, he still could not believe it.

Ruby was the first to speak. "If Lester Walker has been dead all this time, then who attacked us at the Walkers' house?"

"And who has been phoning Josephine, pretending to be Lester and trying to get the locket?" Mick finished.

Ruby bit her lip. "No, none of this matters. The only question, the real question, hasn't changed."

It hadn't. New uncertainties only muddied the waters, but the core of issue was still the same. Where was Alice Walker?

But something else was cutting away at Cooper's insides, a comment, a few words from his brother when they'd told him of the attack by Lester Walker at the cabin.

It couldn't have been him, Peter had said. He'd sounded so certain, as if he knew for a fact that Lester was no longer around.

Cooper felt like sprinting, pounding a path through the forest to find his brother and have his heart put to rest. It was an innocent statement, nothing more. Wasn't it? He tried to tamp down on the doubt burgeoning in his gut.

Mick slid a laptop on the table in front of them. "Pickford was right about Heather. Look."

It was the local online newspaper for their small town and the byline was Heather Bradford, contributing journalist. Inset into the article was a small photo, a sweet smiling Alice Walker, with one front tooth missing.

Cooper closed his eyes for a moment. "Oh, man. I suppose I shouldn't be surprised."

Perry read aloud from the screen.

"'A cold case, decades old, has sprung to life again. The long ago abduction of five-year-old Alice Walker from the Hudson Raptor Sanctuary property has remained unsolved, but a new development may be the key toward advancing the investigation. The discovery of a body by Ruby Hudson and Cooper Stokes in a cave near Sunstone Lake awakened fears and hopes that the child abduction might be solved at last, but an unofficial police source stated that the body was not that of a juvenile, but rather a male adult, who died approximately the same time Alice Walker disappeared.'"

"Pickford is going to have this 'unofficial source' strung up by his thumbs," Mick said.

Perry flicked a glance at Cooper. "'The initial person of interest in the Walker abduction was Peter Stokes. At the time Alice Walker disappeared, police also questioned then 17-year-old Mick Hudson, son of the sanctuary owner. There was insufficient evidence to implicate either man in the crime. Perhaps now, with the grisly discovery, the sheriff's office will be one step closer to finding answers that will serve up justice for little Alice.'" He sighed. "And there's a nice, smiling picture of Heather Bradford, prizewinning reporter."

Cooper shook his head. "She's raked up the whole fiasco again."

"She didn't mention the locket," Ruby said.

"That might give the police a leg up when they do figure out who did this." Mick sipped coffee, eyes shifting in thought.

It was clear to Cooper that the discovery of Lester's body was a shock to all of them. Would it be as much of a shock to Peter?

Ruby got up from the table, her profile determined. "I'm going to check on the kestrels. Cooper's going with me," she added as Mick opened his mouth.

The air grew thick with tension. The Hudsons might as well have plastered their feelings on a billboard. Mick and Perry did not want Cooper to go anywhere with Ruby. Bad seed, trouble. Peter was still the guilty party, the child abductor, the liar.

Yet Mick's name had been mentioned as a suspect right alongside Peter's. There wasn't room for a pious, judgmental attitude from people who were no better than the Stokeses. Worry morphed into anger.

Cooper stood and eyed Perry and Mick, firing off a challenge. "If you want to forbid her from going with me, feel free." He folded his arms across his chest.

Neither man spoke until Perry broke the silence. "We want to protect her."

"Then we're after the same thing." Cooper glared.

"Surely you can understand…" Perry started.

"I understand that you used to be kind to my family, Mr. Hudson. You believed in my brother enough to give him work, to let him tag along with Mick sometimes. I understand that we were all traumatized by a crime that ripped our community apart, and that your son was just as much a suspect at the time as my brother." Cooper let out a harsh laugh. "I guess if I had a daughter, I'd have to ask her to stay away from Mick. I mean, after all, the guy was implicated in a child abduction." Cooper stalked to the front door and slammed outside.

He struggled to get his anger in check, to quiet

the pulse charging through his veins. After a moment, he felt Ruby's hand on his arm. Her cheeks were crimson.

"Cooper, they mean well. It's been a shock, having the whole thing raked up again."

"It's been a shock for all of us."

"Nothing has changed since yesterday when we rode up to the mill together."

Nothing had changed? He knew that Mick and Perry had fully expected that Alice's body would be found and they were hoping for enough physical evidence to put his brother away for life. How could he have let that slip his mind? Ruby was right. Nothing had changed, nothing at all.

He stepped out of her grasp. "We'd better get this excursion going."

"Don't worry about it if you have other things to do," she said, a shade too brightly. "I can manage on my own just fine. I'll make it a quick trip since I have a tour group later today."

He thought about her trembling body pressed to his as the gunshot ripped through the air, her determination to risk it all to go to the aid of her brother. Her impulsiveness could get her killed. "No. It's fine. I need to go into town later, but there's time for a hike."

She nodded and went in the house to fetch a pack and a camera. No doubt she would get another dose of advice from the Hudson men. As he waited,

thoughts racing through his mind like a flock of unruly birds, he saw Mick eyeing him out the window.

He met Mick's eyes and fired back a challenge.
No matter what, I will do what is best for my brother.

The hard stare told him Mick was thinking the
exact same thing about his sister.

They hiked up to the old mill. It was an arduous
trek, but Ruby did not think their lack of conversation was due entirely to the exertion. Something was
weighing on Cooper, no doubt the ugly confronta-
tion at the Hudson home. She wished she could turn
back the clock, back to the time when things were
right. Then again, things had not been quite right
since Alice disappeared.

Even the sights and smells of spring in the forest could not shake away her dark thoughts. They
trudged on, not stopping for more than a couple of
minutes to rest. When they reached the nest box ad-
jacent the old mill, Cooper pulled on a sturdy pair
of gloves and Ruby handed him the camera.

"We could have driven up with a ladder, you
know."

He quirked an eyebrow and suddenly a bit of
cheer returned to his face. "And have you miss a
chance to admire my climbing prowess? I think
not."

She was thrilled to see his smile, the partial return of his ebullient spirit that seemed to infect her

own. In a few moments he was at the top, peering into the hole. "All birdies present and accounted for," he called down. "Chirping their little hearts out. Sorry birds, I came without worms again."

"Take a picture with your phone first. I need to see." In a moment, she had it via his text. Three hungry little beaks all vying for a plump insect or small lizard that Cooper could not provide. She made notes in her pocket journal as Cooper took pictures with the camera she'd given him before he inched back down the pole.

They backed several yards away and sat against the sturdy trunk of a pine to keep watch.

"Let's sit for a little while. I want to be sure Daddy kestrel is keeping up with the job."

"Poor guy. Not easy being a single parent."

She nodded. Wind toyed with the needles above them, releasing a fresh spurt of pine fragrance into the air. "I guess we both know the truth about that. Do you think that's why you and my brother are so protective? Because you both took over the role of a missing parent?"

He cocked his head. "Dunno. I try to imagine sometimes how things would have been different if my dad had lived."

She found her throat was thick. "Me, too, if mom hadn't gotten sick."

"Is it possible we could have had normal, happy

families?" Cooper sighed. "It doesn't pay to wonder about that, does it?"

They held hands, he pressed a kiss to her knuckles and she felt a supreme comfort in the gesture, the warmth of his shoulder pressed to hers. "I'm sorry."

He turned to look at her. "For what?"

"That things are so messed up."

"Not your fault. Life is complicated."

"Are you going to say it's just something we don't get to understand?"

He laughed. "Not if you don't want me to."

"Well, anyway, thank you for being here with me and the birds, in spite of the attitude you're getting from my family."

He raised an eyebrow. "I got that reaction from you, not too long ago. You're still not convinced my brother is innocent, so what's changed? Why are we here now, babysitting birds and hanging out in the woods?"

"I…I don't know."

He swiveled to face her, tracing a finger along her cheek. "Have you finally succumbed to my overwhelming boatload of charm?"

A giggle escaped over the tumult of warmth that grew from his touch. "Maybe I just appreciate your pole-climbing skills."

He was close now, his mouth inches from hers. "And let's be honest, who wouldn't?" Their lips met, and she felt joy, warmth, comfort and longing assault her senses. She found her fingers stroking the back of his neck until they were breathless.

His eyes were soft as he drank her in. "Our families are enemies, you know. I have no business kissing you, but for some reason I can't get you out of my mind."

Bolts of sweetness shot through her, lighting up the dark corners of her heart. "Could it be my boatload of charm?" she whispered.

He laughed and smoothed his thumb over her lips, but something dark nestled beneath the smile.

"You're worrying about something aside from my family, aren't you?" She clasped his hand. "Is it about the police finding Lester?"

Before he could answer, there was a flutter of movement.

They watched as the male kestrel arrived to alight at the nest, tapered wings settling, his beak full of food for his young. They watched in silence as he dutifully doled out the provisions before he spread his wings and took to the air again.

"To find more food," she said, tracking his glorious progress into the blue sky. "When the babies are old enough, he'll take them out to hunt as a family group until they can survive on their own."

"Amazing that he can take all that on."

"It's not an easy job. We've rescued kestrel babies before. They're high-strung and hard to feed, but this male seems to know exactly what he's doing."

The sunlight glinted on the slate hue of his wings and the black bar across his orange tail feathers as he cut through the brilliant sky. Perfect in design, exquisite in motion.

She found herself whispering the words of Victor Hugo that she'd copied in her journal and traced over with every colored pencil in her box. The little poem about the bird that feels the bough give way beneath her but sings anyway, knowing she has wings. Ruby felt at that moment as the kestrel danced through the sky, with Cooper by her side, that maybe for the first time in her life, she really might have wings. "So beautiful," she breathed.

"I couldn't agree more."

Pleasure rippled through Ruby when she realized Cooper was not looking at the kestrel, but at her.

FIFTEEN

Cooper wondered if his sanity was coming apart at the seams. His mind should be fully occupied with trying to sort out his brother's situation, yet it kept pivoting straight back to the auburn-haired Ruby Hudson. He realized on the hike back down from the old mill that he had described to her no fewer than five species of wildflowers as they walked, and was it possible he had waxed eloquent on the difficulties of spotting matsutake mushrooms? Yet she had not appeared bored in the slightest and it somehow fueled his preoccupation. Ruby was a kindred soul, passionate, her heart light and ebullient when she let it be. It enticed him. His brain demanded he focus on his brother, but his heart longed for something entirely different.

Perhaps it was a botany-fueled euphoria that caused him to volunteer to help Ruby lead her tour group when they returned from their hike. Both Perry and Mick were gone, and Ruby was faced with a group of twelve eager birders, one of whom would require assistance on the steepest part of the trip due to a rheumatoid arthritis condition. Though his upcoming conversation with Peter loomed heavy in his mind, he didn't see how a delay would make much of a difference. So, he took his position at the back of the group, trying to blend his six-foot frame in with the gaggle of much smaller females.

It was mostly older ladies from a local birding group, a younger woman with a long blond braid and two teenagers taking pictures of every square inch of the forest and themselves with their iPhones.

He admired the energy Ruby applied to her duty. She was the perfect guide—passionate, attentive, eager to know what particular interests and questions the group shared. He laughed when she stopped at the base of a tree where a cluster of shaggy parasol mushrooms nestled.

"We're fortunate to have a botanist along today. Mr. Stokes, can you lend your expertise here?"

He limited himself to a few short remarks. These were birders, after all, not botanists. They accepted his expertise with good grace, taking pictures and peppering him with questions.

As the group moved along, the woman with the braid hung back to walk next to Cooper.

"You used to live here a long time ago, didn't you?"

He could not guess her age…late twenties? Mid-thirties? Nor did she look familiar. Her eyes were a faded federal blue, face tanned and showing signs of too much sun exposure. The intensity of her gaze kicked his nerves into overdrive.

"Yes, my family lived here back in the day. You, too?"

She didn't appear to hear his question. "I heard about the little girl who disappeared back then, Alice Walker. I always thought she would be found someday." She hesitated. "I read online that the police discovered a body near the lake, but it wasn't her."

Thank you, Heather Bradford. "They're still investigating," he hedged. "If I'm not being rude here, Miss…?"

She did not volunteer her name, just kept staring at him, so he continued. "You seem very interested in the case. Do you have a personal connection to someone involved?"

"Personal? No. I've been thinking about it a lot, is all." She looked up as a startled warbler thrilled the group by bursting out of the brush and flapping away. "The whole thing destroyed so many families."

"You don't have to tell me that."

She raised an eyebrow. "That's right. Your brother was accused. And her," she pointed to Ruby. "She must have been tortured all these years having her friend snatched away and never knowing who took her or what happened."

"And Josephine and Lester Walker."

"Yes, Alice's parents. Still living?"

He nodded, not feeling up to sharing what he knew about Lester. Josephine was living and about to find out the husband she'd thought alive was dead and there was still no sign of her missing daughter. "Mrs. Walker's been wounded most of all."

The woman twisted her braid. "I can only imagine."

He stopped now, putting a hand gently on her forearm. "Do you know something about the Alice Walker abduction?"

She stiffened. "No."

Her pinched mouth and panicked expression telegraphed the lie. "If you do have any information, it's a crime to conceal it."

"A crime?" She took a step back. "I don't know anything about it."

"Then why are you here? On this tour?"

Her mouthed opened, fingers twisting her braid. "I'm interested in birds. Just like the rest of the group."

"I don't think so."

"What do you mean by that?"

"We've been walking for a half hour now and I haven't seen you take a single picture, or use your binoculars once, not even when the two falcons stopped to give us the eye. It's as if you're oblivious to the birds, like you came here for another reason altogether." He tried to catch her eye, but she looked away. "Why are you here?"

"For the birds," she said, edging away toward the group, which was now several yards ahead. "That's all. Do you interrogate all the participants like this?"

He did not push any more. Was his growing paranoia making him see things that weren't there? She was merely a birder like the rest of them. But edgy and uninterested? Asking questions about Peter and Ruby?

Other possibilities surfaced in his mind. A reporter looking for a story? A curious local, nosey for details? Or something else? He realized Ruby had drawn close and pressed her hand to his bicep. "Are you okay?"

"Yes. Fine. Time to split up?"

She nodded. "If you can drive Mrs. Brownley up to the top of the trail in the Jeep, we'll have a look at the eagles." She leaned closer and whispered in his ear, the graze of her lips like velvet against his cheek. "Let's avoid the lake. The police still have the cliff taped off."

He cleared his throat, trying to jostle away the sparks. "Okay. Meet you at the trailhead."

Mrs. Brownley took his offered arm, and he helped her into the passenger seat of the Jeep. Out of the corner of his eye, he saw the woman with the braid watching him. Or perhaps she was taking in the white-tailed kites observing them from the branches high over his head.

"Let's go, Mr. Stokes," Mrs. Brownley said, fastening her sunhat firmly under her chin and straightening the small pack clipped around her waist. "I want to see if you're as good a driver as you are a botanist."

He laughed. "No promises."

She grinned, showing a mouth full of crooked teeth. "I remember when you and your brother used to race your bikes down Sentinel Hill and with no helmets in sight. I hope you've learned some restraint since then."

He started up the car. "So you've been here a long time."

She quirked an eyebrow. "We won't discuss how long."

"No, ma'am. I'm sorry I don't remember meeting you."

"No surprise," she said, holding on as he took the slope. "I was just the bank manager. Not a place a young kiddo would frequent. Besides, I wasn't an old lady then."

"Ma'am, you don't seem like an old lady now either."

"Gallantly said, Mr. Stokes. I will accept your lavish flattery."

He smiled. "So you've been here since…" He

stopped, realizing he might be going out on a potentially offensive limb again.

She chimed in. "Fifty-three years now. I'm like the unofficial historian of this town. I'm older than some of the buildings and most of the residents."

"You must have seen a lot of change, both good and bad."

She frowned. "The worst thing that ever happened was when little Alice disappeared. Josephine Walker used to be a happy soul, energetic and the first to participate in any church doings or bake sale fund-raisers. I remember once she baked one hundred cupcakes with little marshmallow flowers on them to raffle off to raise money for a new steeple. Now she won't even set foot into the church." She sighed. "Tragic, what losing a child can do to someone."

"You knew Lester Walker, too?"

"Oh, sure. Didn't care for him much, a hot head and he could be a bully, but say what you will, he loved his little girl. There was no mistake about that. I never could understand, though, why he would up and leave Josephine, after what she'd been through, losing a child and then to lose her husband. Inexcusable."

Except that he hadn't run away. He'd been lying dead in a cave not three miles from the Walker cabin. It pained him to think that now Lester would be irrevocably lost to her, too. At least before, she could hold out hope that Lester would return. As they pulled away from the rest of the group, he caught her eye. "Mrs. Brownley, do you happen to know the woman with the braid?"

Mrs. Brownley squinted through the thick lenses of her glasses. She peered through the binoculars. "Slim girl there? No, I don't know her."

Maybe she'd driven in from a nearby town. He focused his attention on keeping the Jeep to the smoothest parts of the steep path.

"But I saw her this morning at the library. I volunteer there twice a week. She didn't check anything out, but she asked my help in finding the reference section."

He tried not to sound too eager or too nosey. "Did she mention to you what she was looking for?"

"It was clear she didn't want anyone hovering, so I left her to her own devices in the periodicals section."

"Periodicals?" He forced a smile. "I didn't think anyone read old magazines anymore."

"Not magazines, newspapers. She was looking through old newspapers, really old, some from twenty years ago." Mrs. Brownley stiffened, pointing to a bald eagle, cleaving through the sky.

Cooper did not hear her. Newspapers dating back twenty years. Now why would someone be interested in that?

* * *

Ruby passed around a clipboard at the conclusion of the tour, soliciting comments and inviting participants to sign up for the Hudson Raptor Sanctuary newsletter.

Cooper reparked the Jeep and joined her. He seemed to be scanning the group for someone. "The lady with the braid. Where is she?" he whispered.

"She said she wasn't feeling well, and she left before we started up for the trailhead. Why?"

The worried creases etched into his forehead startled her, but she was busy saying goodbye and answering questions for the departing guests. When she finished, he was rifling through the pages on the clipboard. "Do you have the original registration list?"

"On the bottom. Most people registered through the website, but we take all comers whether they're registered or not, as long as they pay the twenty dollars. Which person are you looking for?"

"The lady with the braid."

"She said her name was Jane, I think."

"Here it is. You hand wrote it so she must have shown up without registering. Jane Brown." His eyes narrowed. "I wonder if that's her real name."

She stood so close he was forced to focus on her. "All right. Out with it. What's your interest in Jane Brown?"

"She was asking questions about Alice and you."

"I think the whole town's abuzz with questions."

"She's not a local, from what Mrs. Brownley says, and she was looking up info in twenty-year-old newspapers at the library."

Ruby's stomach tingled, just a bit. "Reporter?"

"It's possible." He blinked as if coming back to the surface after a deep dive. "It's also possible that I'm becoming paranoid. I'm starting to wonder about myself."

"What else are you worrying about?"

He shrugged. "Never mind. It's nothing."

She took the clipboard from his hands. "It's not nothing." Weighing her words, she paused. Keep it safe and not mention what was on her mind? It was a comfortable strategy and she'd used it often before. Maintain a distance, don't speak of those deeper things that fluttered inside like fledgling birds. But with Cooper she found herself yearning to open herself fully, to let him see and feel and share all her thoughts and emotions and everything that made Ruby who she was. Deep breath, exhaling in a slow, deliberate gust. "I… I've been thinking that Peter was very certain our attacker was not Lester Walker."

Slowly, in painful increments, his eyes swiveled to meet hers. They were not filled with the anger she had dreaded, only a wide river of fear coursing through their depths. "You're going to ask him about it, aren't you?"

He nodded. "I'm sure it's not anything to worry about, but I do anyway. No amount of prayer seems to sponge that feeling away. It's a burden I wrestle with every day."

He looked so downtrodden, she embraced him then, pressing her cheek to his, desiring to ease the pain of the past. "You love him. That's enough."

He clutched at her, pressing his face into her neck, arms tight around her waist. "Ruby, my brother didn't do anything wrong. I've got to believe that."

She was not sure whether he was trying to convince himself, or her. The only thing that mattered was comforting him, taking some of the anguish on her own shoulders. "Do you want me to come with you when you talk to him?"

"I should do it myself, it's my family shame we're dealing with and I should want you as far away as possible."

Her breath caught.

"But I find myself wanting you with me every moment, even when the moments are bad."

His eyes held hers, his grip around her waist gentling, and he leaned down toward her. "Ruby, there is something indescribably beautiful about you that I can't get enough of."

A cascade of longing, fear and sweetness coalesced in her belly. She wanted to say something flip, a clever witticism to break the wonderful, terrible intensity she felt inside. Then his mouth covered hers and his kiss touched her deep inside, in the lonely darkness where no light could find its way. She felt transported to another place where love was stronger than loss.

"I have to find out the truth," he whispered. "And I want you with me."

Though her knees wobbled from the aftermath of the kiss, she followed him as he took her hand and walked toward his truck. Breathing hard and trying to unmuddle the mess of tangled emotions inside, she almost plowed into him from behind when he stopped suddenly.

"What's that?"

She followed his gaze to a scrap of paper tacked to the small announcement board where they posted pictures of the new hatchlings and informational flyers for people to take.

The board was relatively empty now, as she and Mick had been in the process of redoing it when life intervened. Now there was a rectangle of paper, torn from a notepad. Cooper unpinned it and smoothed the crumpled scrap.

"There's a phone number and a message. It says, 'Call' and then…" His face went white, eyes wide.

"What?"

He cleared his throat. "'I know the truth about A.W.'"

SIXTEEN

Cooper did the dialing while Ruby looked on with her bottom lip between her teeth.

The message came up immediately. "The phone mailbox isn't set up. We'll have to text." He raised a questioning eyebrow.

"Ask her who she is and how we can meet," Ruby whispered.

Though he did not think it wise to arrange a meeting with the woman, it would not hurt to have something concrete to offer the police, if the number really did in fact belong to the woman with the braid from the tour. He sent the text.

The minutes ticked by as they waited for a return text. Nothing.

"Do you think it was a prank?"

He huffed. "Some prank. I'm calling Pickford and filling him in." The sheriff's department informed him that Pickford was unavailable and offered to send him to voice mail. He left a message and just as he was about to click the phone off, a text came in.

"It's from Peter," Cooper said, stomach tightening. "So that's why Pickford couldn't take our call."

Ruby pressed his hand. "What is it, Cooper?"

Cooper found it hard to push out the words. "He drove himself to the police station. He says he has something important to say to the sheriff and we need to hear it, too."

Ruby pressed her lips together, face gone pale. "We can't jump to conclusions."

Cold settled deep in his bones. Ruby gripped his hand.

In a fog, he drove directly to the sheriff's office. Ruby did not try to make conversation, and he was grateful. He could not imagine what his brother was telling Pickford, but whatever it was couldn't be good. Through clenched teeth he whispered prayers for Peter's protection.

"Cooper," Ruby said as he pulled into the first parking place he saw.

He stopped, fingers on the door handle. Her eyes were wide and warm, filled with a measure of compassion he had not seen often in his lifetime.

"I just wanted to say, no matter what we're going to hear, you're a good brother and a good man. I was thinking about what you said, that bad things happen and we don't get to know why, but God is there through it all." She paused. "I don't know if I can fully believe that right now, but you've stood by your brother all these years while he disappointed you over and over. I was thinking that maybe God put you in Peter's life..." She paused for a moment. "And it dawned on me back there with the kestrels, that maybe He put you in mine, too. All these years, I've been so focused on Him taking people away, I never thought about it the other way."

It felt like the first rays of dawn, a splinter of light in the darkness. He took her hand and laid his cheek on her palm. The warm, soft comfort of her skin against his. "Thank you."

She pressed a kiss to his head. "You said we'd face the truth together."

He looked at her and bent to capture her lips with his. His thoughts whirled away, leaving only the soft satin comfort of her mouth on his. Together. He would not walk into that police station alone for what might be the worst moment of his life. For that small but precious comfort, he thanked God.

Pulling away, breathless and cheeks pink, she stroked his face. "Are you ready?"

He straightened. "No, but I'm going anyway."

They made their way to the outer office where Heather and Hank rose in unison from their chairs.

"Peter asked me to drive him," Heather said. Her face was tight with strain. Hank put a protective hand on her shoulder. "I tried to talk him out of coming because he'd been drinking."

No. Not that. "With you? Did you toss back a couple to get him to talk for your story?" Cooper snapped.

"No." Hank's eyes were flat with anger. "Heather loves that poor sap, for some reason, as much as I hate the idea."

Cooper blew out a breath. "Sorry. That was uncalled for."

Heather sighed. "It's okay. I know you're worried, too. Do you have any idea what he's insisting on talking about with the police?"

"I wish I did." Again a sweep of dread rippled through him as he and Ruby were shown to a room that Cooper imagined served for both conferences and interrogations alike. Drab olive carpet, plain metal table, four chairs. A plastic pitcher of water and a stack of paper cups, the lingering odor of cigarettes and air freshener.

Pickford came in first and slapped a clipboard down on the table.

"Let me just say I don't want you here, but your brother called a half hour ago and he said he needed to see me immediately. He refuses to talk unless you two are present."

Cooper tried to keep his voice calm and level. "Where is he?"

"They're bringing him in now." Pickford cleared his throat.

Cooper groaned. Ruby gripped his forearm,

but he hardly felt it. Then the door opened and his brother came in under the supporting arm of a police officer. He was not falling-down drunk, but Cooper could smell the beer on him.

Peter shot a bleary glance at his brother and looked away. "I'm here." He collapsed into a chair. "Let's get this over with."

"Fine." Pickford clasped his hands together. "You called this meeting and I've got plenty of other things to do, so I'm all in favor of brevity. Do you mind if I tape record this statement?"

"I don't think…" Cooper started, but Peter shot out a hand.

"It's too late now, Coop. You can't help me anymore. I've got to clear the air. I heard from Heather that you found Lester's body. I can't keep secrets anymore about what happened."

He felt cold despair begin to rise. What was he about to hear? Could he have been so wrong, all these years, about his own brother? No, he told himself fiercely, he wasn't.

"What do you need to tell me, son?" Pickford said, pencil in hand.

Peter sucked in a deep breath. "I have a drinking problem."

"That's not news," Pickford said.

Peter went on as if Pickford hadn't spoken. "I've been drinking since I was thirteen. I've done some bonehead things and ruined my reputation. What happened with Alice only made everyone distrust me all the more."

Pickford leaned forward. "Cut to the chase. You didn't come here today to tell me about your drinking." His eyes were hungry and Cooper realized at that moment that Pickford carried the guilt not just for failing Alice Walker, but the town who looked to him to set things right. "What did happen with Alice, Peter? Tell me."

Peter ran a finger along a scratch on the tabletop. "I was in the woods that day. Ruby did see me, she was telling the truth. I only watched them play for a little while and then I left. Had some beers hidden and I played hooky from work. That's all I'm guilty of. Underage drinking and lying to my boss at the lumber mill about being sick when I should have been at work."

"What about Alice?"

"I didn't touch her, and I didn't see who did."

Cooper's emotions zinged between relief that Peter was innocent, as he'd always believed, and frustration at another dead end, another slammed door that would keep Alice in darkness forever.

"Why lie about it and say you weren't in the woods that day?" Pickford pressed.

"Teen boy, drinking and playing hooky from work." Peter flashed a wan smile. "Easy. I didn't want to get into trouble. I'd told boss man I was sick. Didn't want to get fired if I was caught in a fib."

"So that's it? That's why you wanted to talk to me? You're wasting my time." Pickford got up. "Go back to your dishwashing duties."

Peter almost shouted. "No. I have to tell you the rest. I can't stand it anymore."

"All right." Pickford sank back down on the chair. "I'm listening. What's the rest?"

"My reputation, it's why I didn't tell you everything. I knew no one would believe me. They'd think I did it or I was trying to frame someone else. Who would believe Peter Stokes was telling the truth? I panicked."

Cooper caught his brother's eye. "Peter, just say it. What did you do?"

Meager light picked up the sagging planes and hard lines in Peter's face. He had once been a handsome, fun-loving youth, but now he was a man trashed by years and alcohol, a dull hopelessness in his eyes. "You've always been the guy who believed I had good in me."

The look on Peter's face cut at Cooper's insides. "You did and you still do. I know you did not hurt Alice."

"No one else will believe that. Never, no matter what I say or do." His mouth trembled. "I don't deserve your trust."

"You've got it anyway. I love you, and I'll stand by you, like I always have."

Peter gave an anguished cry. "You're going to change your mind when you hear it."

"Hear what?" Pickford smacked the table with his fist. "Quit beating around the bush and say it."

"I can't…"

"Say it, boy," Pickford thundered. "For once in your life, stand up and be a man."

"All right," Peter shouted. The room crackled with tension as Peter got to his feet, took something from his pocket and flung it on the scarred tabletop. It was an old tan leather wallet, stained with something dark.

Cooper stared. "What is that?"

"It's a wallet I took twenty years ago," Peter said, eyes burning, "off Lester Walker's body."

Ruby felt her fingers grow ice-cold. Off Lester Walker's body. That explained why Peter had been sure it wasn't Lester who'd attacked them at the cabin. He'd known all along that Lester was lying dead in a cave. And he could only have known that if… Her mind would not accept the horror as she watched confusion and fear unroll across Cooper's face. Peter, his brother, the person he'd defended at all costs. She wanted to erase the past thirty seconds, to sponge away the hurt. *Don't let this be happening,* her heart screamed. *Don't let Peter be a killer.*

Cooper started to say something to Peter, but Pickford stopped him.

"Why did you kill Lester, son?" he said, quietly. "Why would you do something like that?"

"I didn't," Peter whispered. "I didn't kill him."

"You knew about his body. Who would know that but his killer?"

"I don't know, but it's exactly why I didn't say anything all those years ago. I knew no one would believe me, not one single soul in this whole town."

Pickford held up his palms. "Easy. Simmer down. Tell me what happened, one thing at a time."

Peter sat and took a shaky breath. "I was out hiking the cliffs."

"When?"

"On Wednesday, a week after Alice disappeared. I thought maybe… I had this dumb fantasy that I would be the one to find her and I'd be the hero. Everyone would be falling all over themselves apologizing for suspecting me." He shook his head. "Stupid kid that I was."

"And?"

"I was hiking like I said, and I came across that cave. In it, I found Lester's body and the wallet."

Pickford leaned forward. "Are you telling me Lester was dead when you found him? You expect me to believe that?"

"It's the truth and I know you don't buy it, which

is why I didn't come to you, why I've never said anything."

"Well you didn't help your credibility by delaying twenty years. So why exactly should I believe you now?"

Peter looked at the table.

"And you just happened to have this attack of conscience today? It has nothing to do with the fact that your brother found the body and now perhaps there's going to be some DNA proof there that you killed him?"

"I didn't. I was in the cave, but I didn't kill him. He was already dead when I got there."

"But you're a proven liar and why should I believe a liar?"

Peter began to rock slowly forward and backward. "I took the wallet because I needed the money. There wasn't much in it, only thirty bucks or so. After I took it, I knew my fingerprints would be on it and I panicked. I hid it away."

"Instead of tossing it? Why? Did you want to keep a memento of your crime? What a tough guy, to steal the wallet of a dead man." Pickford's eyes flashed. "You disgust me. I knew you were scum. All these years, I knew it."

Cooper shot to his feet. "That's enough. My brother needs a lawyer. Now."

"Listen," Peter cried. "You've got to listen. I kept the wallet in case I needed it, in case I was ever accused of killing Lester, just like seems to be happening now."

"No one is accusing you," Cooper started.

"Wrong." Pickford stood again. "I'm doing more than accusing. I'm arresting you for the murder of Lester Walker."

Ruby gasped, unable to believe what was unfolding in front of her.

"No," Cooper shouted.

Peter groaned. "I knew this would happen. That's why I kept the wallet. That's why I hung on to it all these years."

Pickford reached for his handcuffs. "You have the right to remain silent."

"No, wait," Peter cried.

"He needs a lawyer." Cooper took his brother's arm. "Stop talking."

"Step aside, Cooper, or I'll arrest you for obstruction." He snapped a cuff on Peter's wrist. "Anything you say can and will be used against you…"

"But I didn't kill him." Peter was screaming now.

Ruby looked on in horror. All she could think of was how Cooper's heart must be tearing in half that very moment.

"Funny how they all say that." Pickford snapped on the other cuff and hauled Peter toward the door.

"He doesn't know what he's saying," Cooper said. "He's drunk."

"We used a Breathalyzer, and he's not legally

drunk so that's not going to save him." He turned back to Peter. "Anything you say can and will be used against you in a court of law," Pickford finished. "I'm sorry, Cooper, but I've got probable cause and your brother is under arrest for the murder of Lester Walker. I'm certain I'm going to find enough proof in that cave to pin him for Alice, too. It's all going to come out now. You can't stop it."

Cooper started as if he'd gotten an electric shock. Ruby held out a hand to him, but stopped short. How could she comfort him now?

Peter wailed, "If you'd just listen, I'm telling you I didn't kill him. Look at the wallet. Just look at it."

Cooper reached for it, but Pickford stopped him. "Don't touch that. It's evidence."

Ruby peered closer at the wallet, which was stained, she suspected, with blood. It looked familiar. The pulse pounded in her temples.

Pickford called for another officer who held on to the wriggling Peter. He pulled on a pair of rubber gloves and gingerly opened the wallet. His eyes widened, shock loosening the angry lines on his face as he peered at the contents. He looked from Cooper to Peter, before his gaze settled back on Ruby.

"You see?" Peter said. "It's what I've been trying to tell you. The wallet I found there with the body wasn't Lester's."

"What?" Cooper said. "Then whose is it?"

Pickford's gaze once again shifted from the wallet to Ruby.

"It's Mick Hudson's."

SEVENTEEN

A hush fell upon the room as Ruby forced the words into her reeling brain. It could not be Mick's wallet there, soaked in blood, yet it was, she knew it because Mick had made the thing himself, when his high school teacher introduced them to leatherworking. Mick had toiled over that wallet for so long he said he'd never part with it.

But he had. She hadn't noticed when her brother began carrying another wallet. She swallowed hard. "He must have dropped it somewhere, and Lester picked it up."

Cooper rubbed his eyes. "Probably the night he got into a fight with Lester about the eagle feathers. Lester picked it up. Doesn't prove Mick killed him."

Pickford scanned back and forth in deep thought. "Lots of unknowns here. If Peter is telling the truth about where he found the wallet…"

Peter started to answer, but Pickford cut him off. "And if the blood on this wallet is Lester's, how did the wallet get there?"

"Mick didn't…"

"Thing is," Pickford said, staring at Ruby, "all these years we've not been able to find Alice, and now we're closer than we've ever been."

Ruby realized she was holding her breath as the sheriff slid the wallet into a plastic bag.

"Once again, it's coming down to the same two suspects we had twenty years ago. Peter Stokes—" he fixed a hard steel look at Ruby "—and Mick Hudson. Only now, we've got a crime scene to help us dig out the truth." He spoke over Ruby's shoulder to his officer.

"Put him in a holding cell and bring Mick and Perry Hudson in for questioning."

"You can't believe…" Ruby started.

"That your brother is guilty?" Pickford nodded. "That's the thing about this job. I've learned that even the best families can hide the nastiest secrets."

The gleam of satisfaction in his eyes sickened her. "Is this about my brother, or getting back at my father for finding the truth about Molly and not telling you?"

He grimaced. "This is about justice." He held out his palm. "Cell phones."

"Why should I give you my phone?"

"Because I don't want you calling over and alerting your brother that we're coming. Wouldn't want him to suddenly need to go on a long, out-of-town errand or something, and it's better if your father doesn't have the heads-up to prepare a tidy, well-reasoned statement for his son." Pickford's tone dripped with sarcasm.

"You can't do that."

"Oh, yes I can. I'm conducting an investigation and I can prevent you from obstructing that investigation, so give me your cell phones. Now. You'll get them back as soon as Mick's been secured."

Ruby put her phone on the table, and Cooper did the same.

He smiled. "You can stay in the waiting room if you'd like, but you won't be able to speak with your brother for a while. Make yourself comfortable. There's some bad coffee near the front desk. Free refills."

Ruby stumbled out with Cooper's help and found herself sitting, staring at the drab beige walls of the outer room with Hank and Heather close by. Vaguely, she heard Cooper trying to deflect Heather's questions.

"But why are they arresting Peter?" Heather demanded. "What did he say?"

"He knew about Lester's body," Cooper finally told her. "He's known Lester was dead all these years."

She gasped. "He didn't kill Lester."

"That's what he says, too."

Fury pounded so hard in Ruby's head she could hardly hear their chatter. After what seemed like an eternity, an officer handed Ruby and Cooper their phones.

"I want to talk to my brother," Ruby said. "As soon as possible."

The officer shrugged. "Gonna be a while. We'll let you know," he said over his shoulder as he left.

"Your brother?" Heather blinked. "They're bringing Mick in for questioning because of something Peter said?"

Cooper sighed. "I guess you'll find out soon enough anyway. He says he found Mick's wallet with Lester's body."

"Mick's wallet," Hank repeated. "I did not see that coming."

Ruby whirled on him. "He didn't kill Lester. He lost that wallet years ago."

Hank raised an eyebrow. "I just find it ironic. Perry is so good at piecing together evidence, constructing a case against people and now, the police will be doing the same thing to his son. It must gall him." He chuckled.

Ruby nearly screamed. "You hate my father for revealing your own mistakes."

"No," Hank said, thin lips in a tight line, "but I can't help feeling satisfaction that the Hudsons are now the ones under the microscope. Maybe it's true what they say, what goes around, comes around."

"Enough," Cooper said, a warning in his voice. "Time for you to leave."

"Every single detail," Hank continued. "Every tiny moment, every secret you ever had is going to be unfolded and laid out for all the world to feast on." He smiled. "Now your father can see how it feels."

Cooper moved closer, but Hank took Heather by the arm. "We won't be able to see Peter now. I'll bring you back later if he can see visitors."

"Or if he's released," Cooper said.

Hank nodded and led Heather out.

Ruby sank down on a chair and Cooper sat next to her. "This isn't happening."

He took her hand. "I can't believe it either. All these years Peter knew Lester was dead and he never said a word."

"And my brother…" She swallowed against a thickening in her throat. "How did his wallet get there? Lester must have had it in his pocket and now it looks…" She turned to him. "It looks like my brother killed Lester, doesn't it?"

He didn't answer, and his silence spoke volumes.

She pulled her hand away. "He didn't do it."

Cooper nodded.

"You believe it, right?" She was desperate to hear him say so. "You don't think Mick is a murderer?"

Cooper fixed sad eyes on her. "Ruby, for what it's worth, I don't."

She took immense comfort in the words. "It's worth a lot."

"But the truth is sometimes less powerful than the accusation."

"What are you saying?"

He stood and paced back and forth. "People will convict you and your family in their minds, in their hearts." His tone hardened. "Doesn't matter what the truth is. I know. I've lived it, and so has Peter."

"And you blame me. I'm one of those 'people' you're speaking about."

"No."

"Yes." She shook her head, bitterness creeping across her features. "I can see it in your face. We've gotten so close, come so far, but you still hold me guilty along with the town for condemning Peter."

"Am I wrong?" he snapped. "If I hadn't come back and we hadn't shared this week together, wouldn't you still judge me and my brother because of what happened all those years ago?"

She stared at him, cheeks burning, stomach constricted. Was he wrong? Hadn't she and her family cut themselves off from Peter and Cooper like the rest of the town? Was she not at that very moment stepping back from the closeness she'd felt, the love she'd experienced with Cooper because those lines had just been redrawn? Closing the Hudson fortress against anyone who would threaten, anyone like Peter and his brother? "No, you're not wrong." The words burned like acid on her throat. "I learned long ago not to trust anyone except my family."

"I know." He sighed. "But you can't live like that."

"Yes, I can," she said. "I will do what I have to do to protect them."

He reached for her hands. "You don't have to shut me out to do that."

She snatched her hands away. "Yes, I do. You're right, I've condemned you and your family and held on to it all these years. You're right about me. I don't trust people. I never will." She swallowed. "And I can't let myself trust you."

"You got hurt, badly hurt, and it wounded you." His eyes searched her face. "I want to stay with you through this, whatever happens with our brothers."

"But one of our brothers has to be guilty, Cooper. Don't you see that? How can we survive together knowing that one of our brothers will destroy the other?"

He took her then, by the shoulders, and pulled her close, pressing a kiss to her forehead. "That doesn't affect how I feel about you, Ruby."

Her heart fractured into tiny pieces, bitter anguish blotting out the pleasure those words should have created in her heart. "Cooper," she whispered. "You can't have feelings for me. Not anymore."

"Why not?"

"Because if one of our brothers must be destroyed…" Tears ran down her face. "I want it to be Peter."

He stiffened and stepped away. "Ruby…"

"I'm sorry," she whispered. "Something happened to my heart when Alice was taken. It hardened over. You made me feel like I'd gotten past that for a little while, but I haven't. I'm trapped."

He pulled her close again. "Listen to me. God made you to love. If it's not me—" he paused and sighed "—then someone else, but He didn't want you to live your life trapped in anger and fear."

For a split second, she wanted to throw off the bonds of fear and anguish, to let it all dissipate into the vast expanse of sky and grasp instead the sweet freedom Cooper spoke about. To let go of the past, to open up her heart again to faith and love, how tantalizing, how exquisite. But the drab walls pushed in on her, the smell and sound and sights of the place that now imprisoned her brother pressed the hope away. The warmth of Cooper's body seemed to collect the heat from hers, drawing out all that was good and gentle and leaving a cold crust behind. What was happening to her?

I'm afraid to love you, Cooper, she wanted to shout. *Please don't leave me in this terrible place. Stay with me, in spite of it all.* But something born long ago rose up inside her, a chilled stone took the place of her heart, forcing away thoughts of love and a future with Cooper. Instead, she rallied a calm tone, confident and in control. "God's not here, Cooper. Just me, and I'm going to protect my brother, no matter what the cost."

"By cutting yourself off from me?"

She didn't answer.

His eyes shone gold in the waiting room, the only warmth in that horrible, dank place. "It doesn't have to be one or the other."

"Yes," she said, the last piece of her heart dropping away, "it does."

Cooper could not penetrate the wall that rose between them. Ruby would not look at him, nor could he get her to engage in conversation. Those beautiful brown eyes gazed stonily ahead, glimmering with tears that she tried desperately to keep from falling. The tremble in her lower lip made him want to grab her up and whirl her away, to return to the forest where things were pure and simple, where his feelings for her had seemed as clear as the cobalt sky.

Hands balled into fists, he held himself still. He had nothing of comfort to offer since it was clear she had locked him out, as if her fondness for him had never existed. Perhaps he'd been wrong. It wouldn't be the first time he'd assumed a woman felt something deeper for him than she actually did. He'd told her he cared about her at the worst possible time, and managed to make things worse, so much worse. Something burned deep inside as he contemplated her cold profile.

Ruby, he wanted to yell out. *Don't let what hap-*

pened to Alice cut you off from your own life, cut you off from me. But how could he offer such advice when his own experience was colored so profoundly by what had happened that day?

He closed his eyes. *Lord, you showed me there was still life to be lived, people that You put here for me to love. Please show her that, too.*

They remained locked in that terrible silence until Pickford shuffled into the waiting room with Perry Hudson. Ruby sprang into her father's arms, the tears finally trickling down her face. Perry held her, his expression so torn with tenderness that Cooper had to look away.

"Dad," she said. "What's going to happen?"

Pickford answered as he scribbled something on his clipboard. "We're holding both Peter and Mick for twenty-four hours while we finish combing the crime scene. Then we'll decide how to proceed."

"You can't just keep him here." Ruby glared at him. "My brother is innocent."

Pickford cocked his head. "Actually, I can and I'm going to. If you'll excuse me, I've got to go light a fire under the county medical examiner." He disappeared into the back again.

Cooper didn't bother to speak up to Pickford. While he believed his brother had not killed anyone, he had certainly covered up evidence of a crime. The best thing Cooper could do was call around and see if he could locate a lawyer and figure out how to pay for it. There wasn't much left in his bank account after Peter's many stints in rehab and his mother's medical needs. Worse yet, how would he break the latest news to his mother? Worry clawed at his insides.

Perry was saying something about legal counsel when he tuned back in. "I'm going to take you home and make some calls."

Ruby's phone buzzed, and she checked her texts. A frown creased her forehead. "You go ahead, Dad. I'm going to stay here for a while."

Her father shook his head. "No. They won't let you see Mick anyway, Bee, and it's better for you to come home. Nothing you can do here."

"I'll be home in a little while, I promise."

"Why…?"

She kissed him. "I promise."

His look was hesitant, but his body language said he was eager to go, no doubt to start rounding up a legal support team. Cooper did not think the Hudsons had unlimited funds to work with either, but they were probably in a better position than Cooper and his brother. He tried to tamp down a flare of resentment.

When Perry finally moved toward the door, he offered only one further comment, directed at Ruby, though he looked straight at Cooper. "I told you the Stokes family would bring trouble, Ruby. Keep that in mind now that Peter has made his revelation. Look where it's gotten us."

The heat of both anger and shame curled inside Cooper. He had no reply. Peter's actions had implicated Mick, but it was possible, too, that Peter had allowed Mick twenty years of freedom that he had no right to. Try as he might, he could not bring himself to believe Mick had murdered Lester either.

Maybe you're just a naive sap, Cooper told himself severely. *Wouldn't know the truth if it bit you on the chin. Believe everyone who gives you an honest line.* Maybe after blindly believing his brother so many times he'd lost all judgment. The door closed behind Perry, and Ruby stared at it for a while.

"I've got to go now," she said, without making eye contact.

"Where?"

She shrugged. "Doesn't matter."

"It does, and I think it has to do with the text you received."

She jerked. "How did you know that?"

He tried for a roguish smile. "My mad detective skills. Was it from Jane?"

Not a glimmer of a return smile. Ruby's shoulders slumped. "Yes. She said to meet her at Sparrow Valley Junction in forty-five minutes."

"An out-of-the-way spot, isn't it? And you're all set to go running after this lady whom you know nothing about?"

She folded her arms and gave him such a ferocious look that he almost smiled. "I told you. I'm going to do whatever it takes to save my brother. If this woman knows something about Alice, then she might be able to shed some light on what happened to Lester, too."

"And telling the police is out because they already suspect your brother and father and you don't want to make anything worse."

She tipped her chin up. "Yes. So what are you going to do about it?"

He went by and held the door. "Go with you."

"I don't think that's a good idea."

"Unless you're calling a cab, you don't have a ride that I'm aware of."

She arched an eyebrow. "I'll call Molly. She'll take me."

"Maybe, but not without a lot of questions and probably a call to her husband."

She blew out a breath. "Cooper, things between us have changed." Two pink flames kindled in her cheeks. "I can't allow you to help me."

His heart squeezed. "Fine. I'm not interested in helping you, how's that? I know my brother didn't hurt Alice and this is my chance to help him out, maybe my only chance."

She wavered. "She may not know anything. Maybe she's one of those crazy people who follows a story and gets obsessed with it."

He checked the time on his phone. "If we don't get going, we'll never know. It's twenty miles to Sparrow Valley Junction."

"Okay. We'll do this together."

Her tone said it all. *And then I'm out of your life for good.* Ruby Hudson, childhood friend, his brother's enemy, would walk out of his life one more time. Why did it pain him so much to think about it? He'd loved several women over the years, and he'd gotten over each one of them eventually. Why did he have the sick feeling he'd never get over Ruby?

She passed him out the door, her hair brushing against his bare forearm, sending little bursts of excitement through his body. He wondered how long it would take him to stop yearning for the joy that Ruby seemed to have awakened in him.

It's over, Cooper. The sooner you accept that the better.

EIGHTEEN

Outside, Hank sat on the edge of a stone retaining wall, talking on the phone with one hand and working his iPad with the other. Probably looking for a new dishwasher, Ruby thought wryly. Or maybe helping his daughter get out the next installment of her hard-hitting online news story. Had her loyalty to Peter disappeared with this latest revelation? Was her fondness for Cooper's brother just a ruse, a way to get close to him to write the story that might garner her the attention she craved?

Did everyone have ulterior motives, or was it her own rampant paranoia?

Hank gave them a curt nod. Ruby kept her eyes glued to her feet until they got into the truck.

Cooper gunned the engine and they drove away from town, toward Sparrow Valley Junction. The place was not really a destination as much as a turn-off, a shortcut across a mountain meadow that eventually led to the main highway. There was nothing at

Sparrow Valley Junction but a long stretch of road in disrepair, bordered on one side by a thick copse of trees and on the other by a steep drop-off down into Sparrow Falls Creek.

"Weird meeting place," Cooper said, pulling the truck to the gravel-covered shoulder. Trees provided shade from the brilliant sunlight. Rolling down the window he could hear the burble of water from the creek.

Ruby drummed fingers against her thigh. "Not so odd if you were leaving town and you didn't want to take the main road." The thought did not comfort her. It was also a good spot if you wanted to get someone alone.

Cooper checked to be sure his cell phone had reception.

They waited fifteen minutes, Ruby growing more and more agitated. "She's not coming."

"Let's give it another fifteen minutes."

"Why? She's not coming, is she? This is another false hope."

He reached for her hand then, but she pulled away. Her hateful words floated back to her.

If one of our brothers must be destroyed...I want it to be Peter.

"Is there anything else you could be doing to help, other than waiting a few more minutes here?" he asked quietly.

She gathered her hair into her hands and twisted the auburn strands. "I don't think so."

"Then we might as well hang on for a little while longer."

"What if she…?" Ruby's words died away as a blue compact car appeared on the road.

Ruby's pulse sped up. She peered close to try and identify the driver. The car pulled up behind them and onto the shoulder. The woman they knew as Jane Brown got out.

She wore a faded pair of jeans, a baseball cap and sunglasses. Her hair was again caught up in a thick braid. She got out, fiddling with her keys.

Cooper joined her, staying a pace ahead of Ruby, his body between them.

No more protection, Cooper, her heart cried out. *I'm not worthy of it.*

"I'm leaving town," Jane said, twirling the keys around her index finger. "I wanted to tell you something first."

"Is your name really Jane Brown?" Cooper asked.

"No, but that's not important. I saw the article, the online article about Alice Walker and I knew I had to see you."

Ruby wanted to grab Jane or whoever she was and shake the information out of her, but she was afraid the woman would bolt. Biting her lip, she forced herself to remain silent.

"I never meant to hurt anyone," Jane said. "I

didn't know the truth. Honestly. No one will believe that, which is why I'm leaving town, but I never would have participated in anything that would take a child away from her mother."

Cooper nodded encouragingly. "Of course. Whatever you did, I'm sure you had good reasons."

"I thought I was helping." She sighed and shook her head. "I convinced myself of that anyway. Frankly, I needed the money. It seemed harmless as the years passed, but when I saw the picture in that article, I realized..." Her eyes narrowed. "Did you hear that?"

"What did you realize, Jane? Where is Alice Walker?" Ruby nearly shouted.

Jane turned, face frozen in horror as another car approached, driving fast.

Way too fast.

Ruby expected the car to slow as it neared. Instead, the driver accelerated, tires bumping madly on the deteriorated roadbed. Ruby took a step toward Jane, but the woman let out a shriek and bolted for her car.

Still the other vehicle careened on toward them, sunlight glinting off the windshield. Ruby broke free of her paralysis and started for the pickup. Mistake, she realized, as she reached the passenger door. No time for them to escape that way.

"Here," Cooper yelled, grabbing Ruby by the arm and giving her a mighty yank that sent her tumbling into the long grass, separating them. The car, a beat-up Oldsmobile, closed the gap between them, tires flinging bits of rock in every direction. She could not see well over her cushion of grass so she rolled into as small a ball as she could manage, shielding her head with her arms.

"Wait," she heard Cooper yell. Fragments of rock hit her shoulders and back as the car roared past so close she could feel the ground vibrate underneath her.

After it passed, she scrambled to her knees in time to see the car careen into the back of Jane's vehicle with a horrendous metallic groan.

"Cooper," Ruby screamed. In the midst of the collision she had not seen what happened to him.

The impact shoved Jane's small car several yards before it veered off the road. In spite of the crash and the rear-end damage, Jane managed to get the engine started. The blue car shot away, loose fender scraping the ground and releasing a shower of sparks. Seconds later, the Oldsmobile corrected back onto the road and took off in pursuit.

Ruby got to her feet and called again for Cooper. He must have gone after Jane. Had he been hit by the murderous driver?

Her breath froze as she flashed back to the rock slide when she'd first realized how much Cooper meant to her. "Cooper!" she yelled again.

"Here," he called back, rising up from behind a clump of grasses.

Her breath rushed out, heart resuming its erratic pumping as she ran to him and threw her arms around his neck. She wanted to speak, but her rebelling lungs would not allow it.

He squeezed her gently, as if he were afraid to bruise her.

"Are you all right?" she finally managed, murmuring against his chest.

"Just grass stained."

Stained, dirtied, disappointed, she did not care as long as he was whole and unhurt. With difficulty, she detached herself and straightened her jacket. She did not trust herself to stand too close, or lift a hand to his blond hair to remove the smattering of plant debris. He was alive. Her legs were wobbly with relief. Best to stick to the facts of the situation. "Did you see the driver?"

"No. Hat and sunglasses, just like Jane. Small, could have been a woman or a man. I didn't get a license plate number either, did you?"

She shook her head. It had not occurred to her in the past few calamitous minutes.

He brushed off his pants and guided her back to the car with a firm hand on her back. "I don't want us here if he thinks about coming back." He called the sheriff's office as they walked.

He gave one final look into the distance.

"What are you thinking?" she asked.

"I was hoping that whoever that was doesn't catch up to Jane."

Her own reflection was mirrored in the shimmer of his eyes. "We could have been killed. Someone was pretty desperate to keep us from talking to her." Ruby rubbed her hands on her pants.

"I'm worried, Ruby. The rock slide, the stranger outside Josephine's cabin, now this. It's getting serious, way too serious for a plant guy and a bird lady."

She nodded, resisting the urge to smile. "I'll talk it all through with my dad. Maybe he can figure out what to do. He can use his contacts to find her somehow, trace her cell phone number after he's gotten Mick out of custody."

"Your dad might not be enough to protect you."

She stiffened. "He's the only one, Cooper." *I wish it wasn't true, but you can't be in my life anymore. I won't let you.*

They mulled it over further as the truck ate up the miles, Cooper checking regularly in the rearview to be sure the Oldsmobile hadn't made a return appearance.

"Jane participated in something having to do with Alice Walker, something she thought was harmless until she saw the picture in the article."

Ruby pulled it up again on her phone as Cooper drove. "It's a tiny black-and-white photo of Alice, probably taken in preschool maybe. What could it have revealed to Jane?" Her head was throbbing as they pulled into the police station and dutifully waited to report the incident to the desk sergeant. The process took a good hour from start to finish.

Heather Bradford was just getting out of her car along with her father as they exited and made their way to the truck.

"I'm not turning my back on him," she snapped. "I love him and he's innocent."

"He's not. I wanted to believe it, too, baby," Hank said. "I like the kid and goodness knows I've gone to bat for him, but he was covering up evidence, information that would have convicted Mick Hudson, I might add, the real criminal in all this."

"That's not true," Ruby said, slamming the pickup door. "Mick's wallet was at the crime scene, it doesn't mean he was."

Hank shook his head. "Ruby, you're an innocent in all this, but you can't protect your family now. They're going to have to face what they did."

"They didn't do anything," she cried.

"Which is why you'd be happy to pin everything on Peter," Heather interjected. "I heard you talking to Cooper earlier, Ruby. I was in the back room, getting the runaround from a cop. I heard you say…"

"Don't, Heather," Cooper said.

She dismissed him with a raised palm. "I heard you say if one brother had to be destroyed you wanted it to be Peter."

Hank's mouth widened into an *O* of surprise. Shame roiled through her, thick and smothering. How could she be the person who had said such a terrible thing? She did not want Peter to be convicted, but the desperate need to save her brother seemed to smother all rational thought. Again she thought how the words must have wounded Cooper. Heather still stared at her.

"You can't deny that you want Peter to take the fall."

Ruby tried to think of a response. Cooper stepped closer to Heather. "You need to stop this."

"Cooper, your brother has a bad reputation and no father to protect him."

"And he's started drinking again," Hank added.

"Stop." Cooper's voice was trembling with anger. "Cutting Ruby and Peter down isn't going to help anyone. It's wrong and purposeless."

Hank's tone gentled. "Look, Cooper. I was an ally of your brother's. I like to think I've been more than fair, giving him a job, a place to stay when he needed it. For what it's worth, I really did think he was going to hang on to his sobriety, but it's my daughter we're talking about. I can't allow her to throw away her life for Peter."

Heather frowned. "Dad, it's my life, and you don't get to decide that for me."

"That's the father's job, to try and protect. I've

tried to do that but you've been mule stubborn since you were four years old."

She offered a tight grin. "And I don't think it's going to get any better. Now I'm going to go harass the police personnel until somebody gives me information, lets me see Peter or tosses me in jail, whichever comes first."

Hank lifted a shoulder in resignation. "I'll call the café and see if we can bring in some extra people for the evening shift."

Cooper let out an enormous sigh and touched Ruby's arm. "I'm going back to the cabin. Do you need a lift home?"

"No, thank you," she said.

"Ruby…"

"Please," she said, holding up a hand. "Go on home, Cooper. I can't take any more. I really can't."

"I want you to know I don't blame you."

She turned away from the tenderness in his eyes, which she did not deserve. "You should."

NINETEEN

The following afternoon was a glorious one. Though the late-day sun shone in golden splendor, Ruby found she could not feel it, as she perched on a log just outside her office shed, bathed in the dazzling light.

The pencil was in her hands. She meant to make some notes on the baby kestrels who seemed to thrive in spite of the loss of their mother. Ruby had thought she was thriving, too, living out a quiet, but purposeful life in a gorgeous location, with her brother and father at her side, the tragic past a distant memory. The lonely moments were infrequent, the times when she longed for connection with someone who understood her and loved her, faults and all, like her father had loved her mother. Now longing seemed to beat a constant tempo in her heart, eased only in the moments when Cooper was nearby.

It had taken the disastrous discoveries in the past few days to show her the darkest parts of herself, that she would wish blame on his brother if it meant saving hers. Shame and self-loathing burgeoned inside her, but Cooper did not pull away. How incredible, how precious. But the wedge that divided them was too great and he could not see. He had not pulled away, but she had.

Now it was up to her to keep them apart. *Protect your family at all costs, and let Cooper take care of his.* The thought left a trail of bitterness in its wake.

Pickford's police car rolled up the long front drive with another car following. Ruby shot to her feet, dropping the pencil, and dashed to the house, arriving in time to see her father open the door. He still held a phone in his hand and a list in the other— lawyers, she knew, who might be able to help Mick should the unthinkable happen and he was actually arrested.

No, she said to herself as she joined her father. *He's innocent.*

"Hello, Sheriff," her father said wearily. "I don't suppose this is a social call."

"I'm afraid not."

Molly stepped out of the house, clutching a yellow legal pad.

Pickford stiffened. "Just here being a good friend, Molly?"

Her lip curled. "Yes, Wallace. Seems like you're bent on blaming Mick for something he didn't do, so I came to help Perry find a lawyer."

"Of course you did."

Molly huffed. "I've known Mick since he was a child. He didn't kill anyone and you know it."

"I only know what the evidence tells me." The sheriff handed Perry a piece of paper. "Search warrant, for your house and property."

Ruby's stomach constricted. "Surely you can't think that's necessary. We don't have anything to hide."

"It's a legally executed search warrant, which gives us the right to turn this place upside down, if we need to." Pickford hooked his thumbs in his belt. "Sooner you step aside, the sooner we're out of your hair."

"Wallace, no," Molly said. "Please don't do this."

Pickford's face softened, just for a moment. "I'm doing my job, Molly. I owe it to that little girl. Justice is long overdue for her."

Perry stepped outside on the porch and gestured for Ruby and Molly to join him. "He has the legal right. We can't stand in his way."

"Besides," Ruby called to Pickford's back as he entered the house, "you're not going to find anything incriminating because there's nothing to find."

Pickford did not respond. Another officer followed him into the house.

Her father watched him go by, standing there with the phone in his hand. He looked so lost, so unlike her familiar, forceful parent, that she blinked back tears. "Come and use the office shed. You can keep on with lawyer hunting until this silliness is done." She checked her watch. "In a few hours he'll have to let Mick go or charge him, and he's not going to do that."

Molly chewed her lip. "I don't know. He's a terribly jealous man and ever since I…" She shook her head. "Well, I broke his trust years ago, as you both know, and it's never been fixed."

"He can't forgive you?" Ruby asked quietly.

"He says he has, but I'm not sure he knows how to forgive completely. He's not been able to trust that I won't cheat on him again. I think he even follows me sometimes to check up on me."

A thought sizzled through Ruby's brain as they walked to the shed. "The day we found the cave. You two had a fight. Cooper and I saw it from the road."

Her face flushed. "Our dirty laundry sort of exploded, huh? Sorry you had to hear that. Later that day I went hiking around the lake. I had the oddest feeling of being followed."

"You were. I think the sheriff came home and changed his clothes, he took his boat out around the lake, probably to check on you. That's how he got to the rock slide so quickly."

Molly groaned. "This is my fault. I really do love Wallace and I know I hurt him deeply. He will never trust that Perry and I are just friends, and with Hank in town accompanying Heather, well, that's a festering wound to be sure." She sighed. "It's sad to live a life so closed off from everyone who could love you."

"Yes," Ruby agreed softly, grief ripping through her insides, "it truly is." She left the two poring over information about lawyers and stepped back outside, sinking down on the rough-hewn bench where she could keep an eye on the front door. The moment the sheriff and his men left, she would start preparing a coming home dinner for Mick, some soup and crusty bread, a nice salad. It would not erase his humiliation, but it was the only thing she could think of.

Closing her eyes, she tried to find some peace in the sunlight that played across her face. She tried to feel again the joy she'd experienced, the brief moments when she had allowed herself to open up to something greater than the misery she kept locked inside, the tiny span of time when she felt the presence of God. It had been such a soothing balm to put down the blame, the lifetime of guilt. But once Peter had changed the game and her brother was under suspicion, her soul snapped shut tight, impenetrable to God...and to Cooper.

A twig cracked. She opened her eyes to find Cooper standing before her. "You left your cell phone in my truck. Thought you might need it."

"Thank you," she managed. "Is there any news on your end?"

He shrugged. "No. Frankly, I've been avoiding talking to my mother until Peter is formally charged or released. Just delays the pain for a while."

She nodded.

His gaze shifted to the house. "Cops have a search warrant?"

"Yes. Thanks to Peter." She detested the bitterness in her own voice.

"Mick's got to shed some light on things. Can he explain how his wallet got in that cave?"

"He lost it during that tussle with Lester over the eagle feathers. Obviously, Lester was carrying it. Maybe he intended to return it to Mick, but he was killed on his way. The coroner said Lester was probably murdered somewhere else and dumped in the cave before he could hand it over."

He sighed. "Ruby, is there any way we can set our families aside for a minute?" He moved closer. "You're hurting, I can see it in your eyes. We both are. I'd like to pray."

Tears pricked her eyelids. "Why? It won't change anything."

"Maybe not the situation, but it can change the people who are praying."

Something in his earnest tone awakened a need inside her. "I don't think I can do that."

"I've been there, too, thought I could take care of

things by myself, for my brother, and my mother, wanted to shut out God when it hurt too much." He sighed. "Doesn't work out too well in the long run."

"I'm not your responsibility, Cooper."

His eyes grew soft. He stroked a finger down her cheek. "I don't think of you that way."

Her breath caught as he moved closer. His embrace enveloped her tired soul, tingled through the world-weary places inside, yet it was frightening to let him feel that part of her, the naked vulnerability of a little child ensnared by evil on one spring morning. Too close, too intimate. Terrifying. "I'm not a project," she said, jerked back. "Somebody you can fix with prayer," she breathed.

"I wasn't implying that. I just wanted to show you that I care about you. That's all."

"Don't. Don't, because I can't care about you." Her eyes burned, and blood pounded in her temples. Her hands balled into fists in her lap. "I'm too filled up with anger."

"Ruby, listen."

"No." She leaped to her feet. "This can't happen with us. You should go now, Cooper. Go back to your brother."

His shoulders slumped. "I didn't come here to upset you. We have a connection. You mean so much to me."

That golden hue in his green eyes made her knees wobble. Summoning up her last bit of strength, she let the words go that would sever the last thread between them. "You don't mean anything to me, Cooper. Not anymore."

He flinched, mouth tightening. Pain flickered across his face. "That's your anger talking."

"No, it's not." She kept her lips pressed tight together to hold in her own grief. It was for the best. They could not be friends or anything else.

He watched her, strong face tipped to one side as if considering. Then he heaved out a breath. "Okay. Then I guess that's that."

A heart as hard as hers should not feel pain, yet as it cracked in two, the anguish stabbed afresh.

Cooper turned to go as the sheriff came out of the house, talking excitedly to his deputy before he strode purposefully to the little office. Terror pricked Ruby's skin as she hurried to get there. The expression of triumph in Pickford's eyes seared into her.

She was dimly aware that Cooper stood rooted to the spot, watching the situation unfold, but she could not spare a thought for him.

Molly and her father must have heard the sheriff's approach because they both came to the front porch.

"What is it, Wallace?" Molly asked, her hand on Perry's forearm. "You've got a terrible look on your face."

He held up a plastic bag. Ruby could not tell at first what was in it until she pushed herself closer.

"The day Alice went missing she was wearing a pair of blue pants and a hand-knitted gray sweater that her mother made for her." He shook the bag. "Look what we found in the back of Mick's closet."

Ruby stared. Inside the bag was a child-size pair of blue pants and a sweater, clearly hand-knit. Alice's clothes.

"That can't be," Ruby whispered. Her father's face blanched.

"We'll have to wait on the charges for Lester's murder, but for now," the sheriff said, voice loud in the hush of the forest, "your son is under arrest for the kidnapping of Alice Walker."

Cooper's stomach cinched down to the size of a hard fist. He stared at the bag of clothes. Mick Hudson, Ruby's brother, was responsible for the misery they had all endured for the past twenty years? He could not wrap his mind around it.

Ruby turned away, biting her lip, and it was all he could do not to sprint to her and seize her by the shoulders, to press her to him and drive away the awful fear etched upon her face.

Instead he stood motionless, as Perry embraced her, murmuring comfort, low and soft. When he let her go, he pulled out his phone and he dialed.

The sheriff walked back to his car, and Ruby stood alone.

She turned grief-stricken eyes on him. "I guess

your prayers for your brother have come true. My brother will take the fall now."

"It's not what I wanted, Ruby. You have to know that."

Her eyes burned with fire, face a mask of agony. "You go back to your brother and the God who loves you."

"He loves you, too," Cooper said, voice breaking.

"That's a lie." Tears coursed in angry trails down her face. "God abandoned Alice and my family twenty years ago, and I will never turn to Him, or to you. Ever."

She stumbled away into the woods.

"Ruby," he called after her, following. "You shouldn't be alone right now."

She whirled one last time. "Stay away. Don't ever come near me again."

"Ruby," he whispered as he watched her. What was happening? The world was fracturing slowly apart and he could not stop it. Should he be happy that his brother would finally be cleared of Alice's abduction? But how could he be, when Mick's neck was now in the noose?

He drove slowly home, trying to think it through. It was so convenient that Alice's clothes should be found now, after a cursory search. An ugly thought pricked at him. Would Pickford have any reason to plant evidence at the Hudson home? Or someone else? Surely many people might have had the opportunity; perhaps the house was often unlocked and empty while the family was out on their rounds. Molly had regular access, he was sure. Anyone from one of the birding tours could have deposited the clothes.

He burned with indecision. Should he go try to visit his brother? Continue his search for a lawyer? Follow Ruby into the forest against her wishes? Uncertainty weighed down every limb. Her anguish rang in his ears.

Lord, he prayed. *Show her you didn't abandon Alice and her family and you haven't left her either. Reach through her grief somehow.*

He made it home. The cabin was painfully quiet. He tried to eat, tried to sleep, nothing would soothe his mind.

Afternoon slipped into evening. He'd fixed the shelf that had come apart from the wall, split and stacked more wood than his brother would ever need and gone for an exhausting run, more from the hope that he might run into Ruby than any other reason.

When he heard the phone ring at a little after three, he snatched it up.

"Where's my daughter?" Perry demanded.

"I don't know, Mr. Hudson."

"She was upset, distraught after Pickford left. She went to the jail to try and see Mick, but she left there an hour ago and she won't answer her phone."

"Mr. Hudson, I don't know where she is. I'll go check the trail again, and down by the lake."

"No," he barked. "You stay away from my daughter, you and your brother." He clicked off.

Perry would never accept his help looking for Ruby. Perry wanted him gone. Ruby had pushed him away. So be it. Cooper wasn't about to let anything happen to the stubborn, hurting woman who refused to leave his mind even for a single moment. The idea smacked him like a rush of cold wind and suddenly he knew where he could find her.

Grabbing a sweatshirt, he snatched up his keys and ran for the truck.

TWENTY

Ruby watched for the kestrels. Father bird came and fed his little ones and flew away in a flash of lush feathers and the beat of strong wings. She'd always marveled that wild creatures knew instinctively how to care for their young. Perhaps the male kestrel did not grieve when his mate was killed, not in the way that people did, but his devotion to his little ones did not wane, in spite of the hardships. He would soldier on, caring for them, no matter what.

She thought about Cooper, living a life of constant stress and disappointment as he tried to help his brother. Of Josephine, who loved her daughter just as much now as the day she'd disappeared. They both continued to love, in their own ways, in spite of the all the cruelties life had dished out to them. Where did that capacity come from? All Ruby knew was that she did not have it. God had not wired her that way. She was filled with fear and the need for vengeance, not love.

Her eyes went to the nest, the afternoon sun

catching the flickers of movement inside. Tiny babies, tucked in, protected and safe.

Like Alice should have been. *Where are you, Alice? Who took you from the woods that day all those long years ago?* It was not Mick, she knew that with unbendable certainty. Perhaps Peter really was guilty. And maybe he'd gotten Heather to plant the clothes in the house to frame Mick. Would Peter do that? Would Heather? She could no longer distinguish logic from wild speculation.

Restless, she moved away along the path, reaching down to pick up some stones glittering in the shadows. Overhead the trees wove together in a great lacy canopy that blotted out much of the sunlight. Would Mick ever be able to stroll the Hudson Raptor Sanctuary again and see his beloved birds? Would life in prison be the legacy of whomever had planted those clothes in his room? In spite of the best lawyers her father could afford, her brother might not escape the noose around his neck.

She hurled one of the stones into the woods. It smacked hard against a tree trunk. Then the dark emotions thickened inside, and she began to hurl the rocks, handfuls of them, as hard as she could. Frantically, she snatched them up from the ground, flinging the anger and rage and fear with every stone. Ruby kept it up until her arm was sore and she collapsed, panting, to the ground.

"Why?" she screamed to God, tears nearly

choking off the words. "Why didn't you protect Alice? Why are you going to take away my brother now?" She pounded a fist onto the dirt of the path. "Wasn't it enough to take Mom? And then a kid who couldn't lift a finger to defend herself? Now Mick?" She grabbed up handfuls of dirt and flung them at the nearest tree. "You're not good, or loving," she screamed. "You're vicious and I'll never follow you, do you hear me? I hate you!"

Now her body shuddered with sobs, blinded by rivers of tears. Up she scrambled.

The hard earth tore her fingernails as she grabbed up every sharp rock, every piercing twig, rocketing them away with such force that she fell to one knee, sobbing.

Then he was there. Cooper knelt beside her and put his arms around her. She pushed at him, smacked her palm into his shoulder, but he did not let go.

"I'm staying with you, Ruby," he murmured in her ear. "I'm here."

No, no, no, she wanted to scream. She kept shoving at his shoulders, but her efforts grew weak. "Get away from me."

"I'm not leaving."

His arms stayed taut around her, muscles bunched against her struggles. "I'm losing everything," she cried. Grief swelled up her throat until the words came out in a croak. "I'm alone. I'm lost."

He squeezed her hard to his chest, caging her to him. She could hear the fast beat of his heart. "You're not alone."

"You shouldn't be here," she wailed, sucking in gasping breaths. "You can't help me. You can't fix it."

He took her by the forearms and held her far enough away that she was forced to look in his face. "I'm not here to fix it. I'm here to go through it with you."

She trembled in his grasp. "Why?" she whispered.

He smiled and looked into her eyes. "Because that's what we're made to do for each other."

She thought of the kestrel, tending his fledglings, risking his own survival for those weak little creatures.

"I can't turn to God," she hiccuped, "if that's what you're hoping for. He doesn't love me."

He held one of her hands, using his sleeve to wipe away the tears that still flowed down her cheeks. "He does," Cooper said. "Even when you say you hate him."

She sniffed.

"He's big enough to take your anger. So let Him."

She collapsed to the ground and covered her face. "I'm so confused. I don't want to be like this, alone. I feel like I'm lost in the dark."

Draping his sweatshirt over her, he sat next to

her, one arm holding fast to her shoulders. "You're not alone." Wriggling, he pulled his phone out of his pocket and activated the flashlight app. "And you're not in the dark, see?"

She clutched the phone, ridiculously comforted by that small glow in the shadows that seemed to be closing in all around her, by Cooper's gentle smile.

I'm not here to fix it. I'm here to go through it with you.

And there he was, standing firm against her railing, every stone she could throw, every insult she could hurl. Why?

Because that's what we're made to do for each other.

It was all too puzzling and overwhelming. With Cooper by her side, she let the tears flow and her thoughts whirl, grateful for the little sliver of comfort that was all she had to hang on to.

Cooper made sure Ruby texted her father that she was okay. She told him she would be home shortly and she was not alone. No need to add that Cooper was with her. Her father did not deserve any more worry right now. It was after four by the time she managed to stand. Brushing her hands on her pants, she gave Cooper his phone back. "I'm going to the sheriff's office."

"Then we better get started if we're going to get there by closing time."

She caught his wrist. "I'm going by myself,

Cooper. I…I really appreciate what you've done for me, but it doesn't change anything."

He held up a hand. "I understand the situation. The only way through it is to find the truth."

She nodded. "About what happened to Alice."

He opened the truck door for her. "Because it's not going to be finished for Peter or for Mick until we do and the only lead we have is…"

"Jane Brown's cell phone number. That's right, and I have to make the sheriff see that. Jane knows something." She felt a spark of hope.

Cooper frowned. "And someone else does, too. The guy who tried to run us down when we met with her."

"Do you think it's the same person who grabbed me at Josephine's house?"

"Might be, and maybe it's the person responsible for that rock slide." The light reflected off his fair hair and she saw the grave flicker of shadow in his eyes. "I've poked around on the internet to trace Jane Brown's number, but I'm not much of a detective. I tried a reverse cell phone lookup, but that didn't get me anywhere."

"The police could do it easily."

"Only they might not be too motivated to listen to us, since they've already got two people in custody at the moment and we both have a vested interest in protecting our kin."

Ruby tried to pull her hair into a neater ponytail and straighten her shirt. "Then I've got to convince them."

"We," Cooper said.

"No." At the end of the day, she still could not allow Cooper to help her, especially in view of how she felt about his brother. Also, the comfort and ease he awakened in her heart scared her.

He smiled. "Too bad. You've got company on this mission."

"But…"

He waved an airy hand at her. "Besides, you never know when you'll need a botanist. We're very useful people to have around and not just for scoping out mushrooms."

Somehow, against all good sense, she found herself smiling, and one tiny atom of her fear drifted away.

They made it to the sheriff's office before closing time. A man with a head of curly black hair swooped down on them. "Hey, you're the sister and brother of the two accused men. Would you care to tell us your side of the story?"

"No," Cooper said.

"Come on. Just a quick comment."

The man readied his iPhone to take a picture. Cooper blocked the camera with his forearm.

"No comment," Cooper growled, "and no pictures either."

"You can't do that," the reporter said. "This is a public building, and I can take pictures if I want."

"Get out of our faces." Cooper stayed ready, standing in front of Ruby in case the guy tried for another shot.

Pickford emerged from the back room. "Awww, I'm too tired for this stuff. Harold, get out or I'll arrest your sorry self."

Harold glared. "You can't…"

"I don't care at this point. I've got a badge and you don't. Get out or I arrest you and put you in a holding cell until morning, after I confiscate your iPhone, of course. No guarantees it won't accidentally get stepped on in the process."

Harold shot one last glare at Pickford and then he turned to Cooper. "Like it or not, you're news. Might as well tell your side. Here's my card." He held one out between two fingers.

Cooper folded his arms across his chest. "Keep it."

Harold shrugged. "Suit yourself, but I'm not the only reporter around sniffing out a story." He pushed through the doors and left.

"If you're wanting to see your loved ones, the answer is no," Pickford said, "like I've already explained to Heather and her father and Perry and Molly and anyone else who has asked. No one is seeing Mick and Peter until I've questioned them thoroughly."

Behind the counter, Cooper saw the bustle of busy cops coming and going from the back rooms. Interrogating his brother? *Peter, give them the truth, all of it.*

Ruby put her hands on the counter, small against the ugly gray Formica. "We want you to trace Jane Brown's cell phone number. She knows something about Alice."

Pickford quirked an eyebrow. "Brown? Oh, yes, the woman who you arranged to meet before some guy allegedly tried to run you down."

Cooper gritted his teeth at the sheriff's obvious disbelief. "Can you run the number?"

"Sure. When we get the time, in between handling Lester's murder and your kinfolk."

"It needs to be done now," Ruby cried. "There's a lot at stake."

"I'm sure there is," Pickford growled, "but at the moment, we're busy processing two suspects and reopening a file that's been cold for twenty years. Forgive me if I don't drop everything and follow the directives of the suspects' siblings."

Ruby gasped. "How can you turn your back on this?"

Pickford's eyes blazed. "I'm not turning my back on anything. We will follow up that lead, like every possible lead, methodically and thoroughly, even if the timeline isn't to your satisfaction."

"Then I'll ask my father to investigate. It's what he does, after all."

"If your father puts his nose in this case, I'll have him arrested, too."

"A reporter could do it," Cooper snapped. "We could go to the press."

"Harold?" Pickford laughed. "He writes for a rag mag and he's not interested in the facts, only the splashy headlines. If you want to waste your time with him, be my guest, but don't blame me when it blows up in your faces. Now, I've got to get back to work." He trudged off, leaving them standing at the counter as the police business hummed along around them.

Ruby shook her head. "If they delay, we might never find her again. Maybe I should ask Dad."

Cooper mulled it over. "Let's try another way first."

"Do you think we should call Harold?"

"I've got a better idea. What about Heather?"

"Heather?"

"I'll bet she's got a source who could trace that number."

Ruby's stomach tightened. "Heather will be glad to see my brother put away. I don't want her help. I'd rather ask my father."

"You heard what Pickford said. Anything he comes up with will be discounted as Perry trying to protect his son."

Cooper remembered the wild note in Perry's tone when he had called looking for his daughter. It was not the time to send him chasing the elusive Jane Brown.

Ruby's brow furrowed. "I don't know."

"Heather is the best chance. She said she wants closure for Josephine, and that's not going to come until…"

Cooper had not realized until then how loud he was speaking. There were several people seated on the dingy upholstered chairs in the waiting room. Fortunately, most were engrossed in their cell phones and one was hidden behind a two-day-old newspaper.

She stepped closer to him. "Until Alice's body is found. Isn't that what you were going to say?"

He sighed. "Yes."

She swallowed hard. "Do you think she would do it? I don't know if I trust her. She'd do anything to help Peter."

"If we ask, and she says no, then we'll have the answer about whether or not she really wants to dig up the truth."

Cooper watched Ruby's eyes shift as she thought it over. What did she have to lose? Her brother had been arrested for abducting Alice Walker. If Heather got them nowhere, her next move would be to put it before her father.

She sucked in a deep breath and let it out. "Okay. Let's call her."

Cooper looked at his phone. "My phone's dead. We'll have to call from the cabin."

He held out a hand for Ruby. "Are you ready to go?" He waited to see if she would take his hand, to accept his crazy idea that might get them to a truth that would truly rip them apart forever. If his brother had been lying all along…

If Mick had deceived his family…

Cooper's mind spun with dizzying doubts until he pushed them away. *The truth is that God's in charge and you're here for Ruby. Hang on to that and get moving.* But would she go with him, after so much hurt and so many years of seeing the dark side of the world around her?

After a moment of hesitation, she put her small, cold fingers in his. "Okay. Let's go."

His heart leaped as they left the police station behind them.

TWENTY-ONE

Cooper kept to the speed limit by sheer force of will. A strong feeling took hold of him that Heather was the one who could unlock the mystery. She was skilled at digging, tenacious as an eagle after a trout. He knew he could convince her to do it if she felt it would not harm Peter in any way.

As soon as they reached the cabin, he ushered Ruby inside and went for the charging cord, breathing new life into his cell phone. He called Heather's cell phone twice with no answer so he sent a text message. Then he searched out her work number on the internet and left a voice mail. Short and sweet. "We need you to use your contacts to find Jane Brown. Pronto. She knows the truth about Alice." He added her cell phone number.

A buzz startled him.

"Ruby, it's a text from Heather."

She blinked. "Did she get your messages?"

His heart thudded. "It says, 'Doesn't matter anymore. At lake.'" He stared at Ruby. "'Found Alice.'"

Ruby's mouth dropped open. "How? Where? Is it… Is she…?"

Cooper texted follow-up questions as fast as his thumbs would move. There was no answer from Heather. He paced the floor, riveted on the maddening gadget. No answer but lengthening silence. "I'm going to go meet her at the lake."

"We're going to go," Ruby fired back.

He stopped pacing. "There's something weird about this text. It doesn't feel right. You go home and I'll call you when I know something."

Ruby folded her arms; a flicker of fire danced through her expression. "Uh-uh. You said 'we' and 'You're not alone' and all that. Was that just talk or did you mean it?"

Her steely-eyed determination did something to his insides, made his pulse beat up-tempo like a silvery jazz song. It was a more intense version of the feeling he got when he saw the perfect flower—rare, precious, exhilarating. She was perfection, angry perfection. "I meant it, but…"

"But only when things were going well and there was no risk involved?"

He gave her his most ferocious frown. "Be sensible. Rock slides. A knife to your throat. Gunshots. Nearly being run down. Isn't that enough to convince you to stay back? I know it would convince your father," he added quietly, "and your brother."

It was three words too many.

She glared, chin up, head tossed back and copper strands flying loose from her ponytail. "My brother is in jail. So is yours. It's now or never, and it's getting late so accept your fate and quit dillydallying."

He sighed, hiding a smile. "All right, ma'am, if you're sure."

"Completely sure."

"Then let's fly."

"I don't see her car." Ruby peered through the windshield into the dusk. The lake was quiet, the birds settled into their leafy hideaways, or resting on the banks. The water rippled in the moonlight, as the spring breeze set the lake and the branches of the massive pines all around them dancing.

"She might have hiked up," Cooper said, tucking a flashlight into his pocket and handing her another. He'd managed to charge his phone a bit in the car as they drove.

They got out and he texted her again. The reply was quick.

At trailhead.

"There," Ruby cried out, pointing to a faint light shining at the base of the cliff.

Cooper texted again. What did you find?

The truth. Police on their way. Taking photos.

He texted again, but there was no further response so he pocketed it and turned toward the path that circled the lake.

"Cooper," her arm shot out and stopped him.

He turned curious eyes on her, hopeful, maybe, that she had changed her mind about the clandestine meeting. "Do you want to wait here for the police?"

"No, I want to be there, if it really is Alice." The moonlight painted her face in luminous beauty, catching the tenderness and the grief etched there. "I think this is it. After all these years. Alice, little Alice." She wanted to continue but her throat thickened. A need nearly overwhelmed her. "Can you, could you please pray that whatever we find will bring Josephine some peace?" Tears rolled down her face. "She's been tortured," she stopped, gulping back tears. "There's nothing in this world that can make that right."

Cooper gathered her in his arms, wrapped her in a tight embrace and poured out a prayer for peace, for closure, for Josephine and Ruby, Peter and Mick, and all of the people who had been hurt. The soft syllables rolled through her.

"And God," she found herself gasping in Cooper's chest, "please let us heal, all of us."

He kept her there after the *amen,* allowing her to soak him with her grief and somehow in the space of a moment, it was bearable. The anguish lifted off her shoulders and up to God, and here was Cooper to comfort and bear the remainder with her. In the space of a moment, her life was changed.

She tipped her wet face up to his and kissed him, gently, tentatively asking with the softness of her lips for forgiveness from this man, whom she had wronged.

He kissed her back, stroking her hair, covering her in a gentle sweetness that whispered through her with the cool refreshment of the spring breeze. When they ran out of breath, she looked at him, and traced a finger down his temple and his strong jaw. "You are a good man, Cooper."

His smile dazzled her as he stroked her shoulders. "Takes a good man to keep up with an incredible lady."

She did not understand how he could possibly think her incredible, after everything that had happened. Rather than trying to puzzle her way through it, she simply gave him her hand and they walked along the moonlit trail, heading side by side toward the truth.

Cooper marveled at the fact that the human heart could feel both joy and grief at the same time. His soul was light, buoyed by the prayer he'd shared with Ruby, awed at his tender feeling for her, and at the same time weighed down with the heavy mass of what lay ahead.

He kept tight hold of her hand and by some unspoken agreement, they walked in silence. When the path became too narrow, he eased in front, making sure if there was some way to shield her from the pain of discovery, he would be able to do so.

It was cold now, his shirtsleeves did not protect him from the chill, but at least Ruby had acquiesced to wearing the sweatshirt. The light in the distance became sharper and clearer until they came to the ragged pile of rock at the cliff bottom and found the flashlight wedged there.

"Heather?" Cooper called.

"Not Heather," a voice said, and Hank Bradford appeared from behind a boulder.

"Hank?" Ruby said, peering around Cooper's shoulders. "Where's Heather?"

"Driving all over town looking for her cell phone, I'd imagine." Hank wiggled the pink device between his fingers.

Cooper's nerves fired to life. "You were at the sheriff's office, the guy behind the newspaper. You sent us those texts pretending to be Heather."

Hank nodded gravely. "Had to be done."

"Why?" Ruby said, eyes wide. "What do you have to do with Alice Walker."

"Everything, I'm afraid," he said, taking a gun from his pocket.

* * *

Ruby tried to force the reality into her brain as Hank urged them up the trail, gun trained steadily at their backs.

"I couldn't let you contact Heather to trace that cell number."

"Why?" Cooper said. She marveled at the steadiness in his voice. "Because she'd figure out Jane Brown's real identity?"

"She already knows the woman. Jane Brown is Diane Leonard, Diane Victoria Leonard."

Ruby stopped breathing because she knew whatever was going to come next was a game changer.

"She's Heather's mother."

Something dark and cold slithered along Ruby's spine as she heard the rest.

"Or the woman Heather thinks is her mother. I paid her. Gave her a story about my wife leaving and how the poor kid needed to believe she had a mom. Jane is not a rocket scientist, but I guess she finally figured out the truth."

Cooper sighed. "The woman you were speaking to on the phone, the one I thought was Molly. It was Diane."

Ruby remembered Heather's earlier lament about the woman who hardly had time for Heather, who had supposedly walked away because of Hank's infidelity.

"Why would you...?" She thought about the

article that Jane had seen. The picture that had rattled her. There were two pictures included, one of Alice as a little girl, and the other...

Ruby stopped dead. "Jane realized that Alice and Heather are the same person when she saw those pictures together." She turned on her heel, heedless of the gun pointed at her. "You took Alice." Her body went numb. "You took her all those years ago. Why?"

Hank's face went from remorseful to rage filled. "I wanted to punish your father for ruining my reputation in this town. After he outed me as Molly's lover and a thief, I was finished here. I had to move away, I lost everything."

"But how did taking Alice fix any of that?" she gasped.

"I didn't mean to take her." His eyes narrowed as he stared at her with a look that turned the blood in her veins to ice. "I meant to take you."

Cooper could not put all the pieces together, but he figured he had the big picture. "Lester found you, somehow knew you took his daughter. What were you going to do? Kill her?"

"No. I was just going to hang on to her for a while. Make Perry suffer. I was gonna skip town and drop her somewhere in the middle of nowhere on my way to some foreign country where no one would ever find me."

"But your plan didn't work," Ruby whispered.

Hank nodded. "After I snatched her, I stuck her in the trunk of my car and drove to my place. Didn't take long to figure out I got the wrong kid."

He leveled a hateful glare at Ruby.

"Why didn't you let her go? Just leave her in the woods where she could be found?" Ruby said.

"Because she was old enough to tell the police who I was." He sighed. "I wasn't sure what to do. I locked her in the bathroom and joined in the search to keep suspicion away, but I found her locket in my car. I decided to toss it in the lake so maybe people would think she drowned. Lester saw me with it. He went bananas. I tried to fend him off, hit him in the head with a rock a little too hard. Had to put him in the cave and hope nobody found him. I had no idea he was carrying Mick's wallet." Hank flashed a smile. "If I had known that, I'd never have started a rockfall to keep you away from the cave." He grinned.

"Or planted the clothes in Mick's room," Cooper added. "Why frame Mick now? All these years you were happy to let the suspicion rest on Peter." Cooper tamped down on the anger in his belly at the thought of what Hank had done to his family, to Ruby's, to the Walkers. All in the name of revenge.

Hank gestured with the gun. "I'm not a bad guy. I felt terrible that Peter was blamed. I tried to make it up to him by giving him a job when he came back to town. Heather grew fond of him, unfortunately. She contacted him initially because, as much as I dissuaded her, she wanted to solve the Alice Walker mystery." He shook his head. "Ironic. She was trying to solve her own disappearance, and she didn't even know it. I could not talk her out of it, so I came along, to keep her from finding out the truth. Everything started unraveling when that locket turned up and Jane threatened to tell what she knew. I had to try and quiet her, so I tried to run her down."

"You stole a child. You brainwashed her into thinking she was yours," Cooper said. "How did you do it?"

"She was young," Hank said, almost wistfully. I told her her parents were gone. I just kept telling her and telling her. My place is remote, so there wasn't a chance anybody would guess. After a while, she just accepted as truth, what I told her."

"You took her away from her real mother and father," Ruby said.

"Shut up," Hank snarled. "This is because of your father, don't forget. He deserved to be punished and now he will be. I thought I got over that need for revenge. I've been a good father to Heather and I was content to be her dad and run my little café, but since it's all blown up again, I have no choice. I can work out a happy ending for both of us."

"Happy ending?" Ruby said. "How so?"

"Mick goes to jail. Peter is cleared." He smiled.

"Perry loses one son to prison and his daughter and her boyfriend to a terrible accident."

Accident. Cooper's insides quivered with desperation. Hank couldn't win. It wasn't going to happen. He needed to find a way out.

"Heather's going to figure it out. One day, she'll know the truth."

Hank grunted. "I'll deal with that when it comes up. By some twist of fate, I took the wrong kid, but Heather is mine, my child, just as if she'd been born that way."

Cooper marveled at the twisted thinking. "Why'd you shoot at us that day at the mill?"

"I slipped into the hospital and Josephine thought I was Lester. She explained where she hid the locket. I wanted to destroy it, before Heather got a look. I was afraid it might jog her memory. I tried to get it earlier at Josephine's, but I couldn't find it. Went after you with a box cutter, Ruby. You were both stupid enough to think it was Lester." He kept them moving up the steep trail. "I'll bury the locket when I have the time. No chance that it will resurface again."

"Where are we going?" Ruby said. She stumbled, and Cooper turned to help her over a log that crossed the trail. Her voice was calm, but he could see the fear in her face. He squeezed her fingers reassuringly.

"Just over this peak and down into a little gulley.

The police have cleared out. You came up here for some reason. To be alone, maybe?" He laughed. "You two seem to be getting along like peas in the pod."

Cooper's hands twitched.

"Or maybe to see if you could find some evidence that the cops couldn't, to try to clear your brothers' names." Hank told them to turn down a narrow sliver of trail. He remained at the top, gun pointed at them.

Cooper slipped and slid, trying to help Ruby, but not able to keep his own footing very easily. It was going to be a rock slide, only this time, Ruby would be caught in it, as well.

How could he prevent it? What could he do?

They reached the bottom, a place where the crystal-flecked walls pinched together. There was almost no vegetation, just a twisted pine, gnarled and aged, silhouetted against the sky. Hank told them to stop.

Cooper put Ruby behind him. "Heather thinks you're a good father. How are you going to live with yourself knowing you killed the woman who was her best friend?"

Hank twitched. "She doesn't even remember Ruby."

"Oh, yes, she does. She has memories of her true identity. Somewhere deep down, she recalls playing in the woods that day and she remembers her mother, Josephine."

"Enough." Hank backed up a few steps and positioned himself behind a boulder. "She's not Alice Walker anymore." There was a naked longing on his face. Hank Bradford, twisted though he was, really did love the girl he'd taken.

"Yes, she is," Cooper shouted. "You can't change who she is."

"No," Hank rasped, grunting as he shoved at the rock.

"She's Alice Walker." The name echoed through the canyon and bounced across the lake. "Alice," he screamed one more time.

Hank yelled something and kept on pushing, but Cooper's shouts reverberated, echoing back to the man who had stolen the name of an innocent child.

Ruby frantically searched for a way out. Cooper was doing the same, she knew. Now was the time, while Hank had to pocket the gun as he pushed, maddened to hear proof of his sin echoing through the air.

The tree. They both seemed to fix on it at the same time. The branch was some seven feet above their heads. It was the only way.

Cooper linked his fingers. "Here, up. You've got to reach it."

He hefted her up as high as he could, but she

couldn't do it. Cooper changed gears and jumped up himself. Wrangling like a clumsy bear, he tried to get a leg up. It took two tries before he made it and hoisted himself.

The trickle of rocks had started and Ruby felt the ground shake as the giant boulder popped loose.

Cooper braced on his stomach, lowered his arms down.

"Grab on," he screamed over the flood of debris.

Ruby stretched until her vertebrae cracked, but she could not reach. He wriggled lower on the branch, and she could see him straining every sinew, but there was no way he could reach her.

The wall of rock rushed toward him.

"Cooper," she screamed. A spatter of rock particles peppered her face, and she instinctively looked away from the roaring tide.

TWENTY-TWO

Cooper forced his eyes open again. Ruby was not there. He looked into the tumult of rock, the tons of shifting debris that flowed mercilessly only inches below. Dirt billowed around them. He clung to the branch, eyes burning for any sign of her.

The sliding earth slowed, piling up nearly to the branch to which he'd clung. His stomach convulsed in fear. Where was she?

A strange noise filtered down from the top of the trail, but he paid it no mind. He could not fear Hank and worry for Ruby at the same moment. He wiped the grit from his eyes with the back of his hand. "Ruby," he called, but only a cough came out.

Vaguely he was aware of movement behind him. Arms aching, he craned his neck.

Ruby appeared on the branch next to him, face covered in dirt. A grin split her face.

"Climbed up the trunk instead. You're not the only one with skills."

He felt his limbs grow so weak, he nearly tumbled off. "Ruby." Relief purged every other feeling from his body.

She gave him a cocky nod. "Now you can appreciate *my* excellent climbing skills."

He sucked in a grateful breath and craned his neck. "I don't see Hank, but…" he started, eyes wide in surprise. "Hang on. It's okay. Come on, we can get down now."

They clambered down together.

The ground shifted under their feet and they half walked, half crawled back up the slope. He, holding her arm in some places, and she, giving him her hand when his feet could not find purchase on the unsteady pile.

"Are you sure Hank isn't waiting at the top still?" she panted.

"Yes, Pickford is there, and Hank is handcuffed." Grateful as he was that Hank was in custody, he was more grateful still that Ruby was around to see it. He thanked God that another precious woman's life had not been snatched away.

When they scrambled up to the path, Pickford was indeed reading Hank Bradford his rights, but Ruby hardly paid any attention because Heather— no, Alice—was there, staring in mute horror at the man she had thought was her father. She looked at Cooper and then her gaze swiveled to Ruby.

Something inside Ruby ached for the betrayal she

saw in Heather's eyes. She reached out a hand, but stopped before she touched her.

"You two okay?" Pickford called, not unkindly. "Saw you made it to the tree. Need an ambulance?"

Cooper shook his head. "No. How did you find us?"

Heather began speaking, her voice oddly without emotion. "Got your message on my work phone. I was there looking for my cell. Dad…Hank took it from my bag while I was in the back at the station, trying to badger the cops into letting me see Peter. I called my contact and he traced Jane's number quickly."

"And you realized Jane Brown was the woman you thought was your mother."

"She and Hank have been lying to me my whole life. I went to the cops. While I was there, Jane called the sheriff's office and told them that she suspected I was, I am, not Heather Bradford. Pickford pinged my cell phone and we followed the signal from the last text here, to Sunstone Lake." She gazed at Ruby. "So I'm Alice Walker. I'm the girl who disappeared in those woods twenty years ago."

Hank opened his mouth, then closed it. "You're not Alice anymore."

She stared at him, with the hopeless look of a drowning woman.

He tugged at his handcuffs, as if he meant to

shuck them off and throw his arms around her. "I'm your father. The past doesn't matter anymore."

"Doesn't matter anymore?" Heather echoed. Her gaze swiveled to Ruby.

"I'm so sorry about what happened," Ruby whispered. "But I'm not sorry you're alive."

She spoke slowly, dreamily. "All those years ago we were together, playing our little-girl games in the woods. And then in one single moment, everything changed. Why can't I remember being Alice?" Heather looked at Hank. "You stole my life, and my identity."

Hank's tone was pleading. "I gave you a new life, a better one. I gave you everything. I am a good father. I took you away from crazy Lester and a poor family that couldn't give you enough."

"And who gave you the right?" Her face blazed with anger. "Why do you think you had the authority to decide that I shouldn't be Alice Walker anymore?"

"You are better off being Heather Bradford."

She shook her head. "The sheer ego, the self-inflated pride. How come I didn't see it before?"

"You're better off…" he started again, but she cut him off.

"Why would I be better off with a child abductor, an adulterer and a thief?"

Each word made Hank flinch, and he shuddered

visibly. "You grew to love me," he said. "You can't deny that. You love me."

"Well things can change, can't they?" she said. Her voice dropped to a choked whisper. "You are not my father."

"I am," Hank cried. "You will understand, if you let me explain. They are poisoning your mind, the Hudsons and Pickford. You belong to me."

After one long look, Heather turned her back on him.

"You belong to me," he screamed again.

Pickford grabbed him by the arms and handed him to a deputy. "You've had twenty years to talk to her. Now it's over."

Hank shouted and thrashed, but the officer held him steady and he was hauled away.

Heather watched until they disappeared out of sight. Pickford cleared his throat. "I will wait for you at the trailhead. Take your time." He turned to go and then stopped. Grief pulled at the edges of his mouth. "Alice, I just want you to know that every day of my life I've kicked myself. I failed you and your mother. If I had been a better cop, maybe you wouldn't have lost twenty years. I'm sorry."

With shoulders slumped, and head bowed, he left.

Heather stared at the ground as if she were trying to figure out which planet she had landed on. "I don't know who I am."

Ruby looked at Cooper and he gave her a nod of encouragement.

"I know who you are," Ruby said, stomach fluttering. "You're Alice Walker. You are imaginative, loyal, fun loving and determined, and we were best friends."

"That's who I was." Her voice was flat. "Yesterday, I was Heather Bradford and today, I'm someone else. Who am I now?" Her eyes seared into Ruby's. "Who am I now?"

The words hung in the air, humming with the desperation of someone who'd had everything snatched from her hands by a vicious, howling evil.

Ruby swallowed. "This is going to be hard, so hard for you. I can only imagine all the things you're going to have to reconcile in your mind and heart." She moved closer. "Alice…"

"Don't call me that," she snapped. "I'm not…" The air leaked out of her and her face crumpled. "I don't know who I am."

Ruby took a deep breath. "I can't fix anything, but, if you'll allow me, I will walk through it with you."

Alice stared at her.

Ruby held out her palm.

Slowly, tentatively, Alice reached out her own, and after twenty years, Ruby joined hands with the friend she had lost and found.

* * *

It was a week later that Cooper, Ruby and Alice gathered on the rickety steps of Josephine's cabin. There had been numerous tumultuous meetings between Ruby and Alice, and Cooper couldn't be prouder of Ruby for her calm and steadfast support in the face of Alice's tidal wave of emotion. At Alice's request, they were with her when she prepared to meet the stranger who was her mother. Ruby, along with Pickford and a psychologist from the hospital, had met with Josephine to explain the inexplicable. Ruby was not sure how much Josephine grasped, except for the giant, glorious truth that her daughter Alice had finally come home again.

Cooper checked his watch. Ten thirty. Peter had been attending an A.A. meeting every morning faithfully since the police had released him with no charges. He was maintaining the sobriety he'd clung to steadfastly, except for the day he'd been arrested.

"I'm going to beat it every day because Heather..." he'd said, shaking his head. "I mean Alice needs me. We're good for each other."

Much to Cooper's surprise, he agreed. In the face of Alice's life-altering revelation, Peter had been a strong and steady support. Cooper didn't fool himself into thinking it would be smooth sailing from now on, but he thanked God that Peter was truly committed to his sobriety and to Alice. *It's not your job to save him,* he reminded himself. But maybe, this time, Peter would be able to save himself, with God's help.

Josephine opened the door, blinking. Her expression was clear of the confusion she'd experienced in the hospital. Alice took a step back, face pale, but Ruby reached for her hand. "Mrs. Walker, this is your daughter, Alice."

A smile more dazzling than an Oregon sunrise broke over Josephine's face. Her mouth trembled and gently, she touched her fingertips to Alice's cheeks. "I knew you would come home, baby. They told me to stop believing, to give up hope, but I never did. I knew you would come home one day." She clutched her daughter in a hug, tears streaming. Alice's face went from fear, to shock, to the tiniest flickering of joy, as she returned her mother's hug.

Cooper wondered if it meant something for Alice to know she had been wanted, grieved over, mourned and, above all, loved for all the precious days of her life.

They went inside and Josephine produced a tray of cookies. "Oatmeal raisin, you always loved oatmeal raisin," she clucked.

A bemused half smile flitted over Alice's face. "Yes, I do love them. I wish I could remember more. I just have vague memories of climbing in a big tree and a tall man with a beard. I thought they were dreams."

"That was your father, Lester." Josephine smiled, produced a photo album and seated herself next to her daughter. "They told me you might not remember much at all. Here are some pictures." She looked uncertain, twisting her hands together. "Do you... do you want to see them? We could look later, if you don't feel right about it now."

Alice cast a panicked glance at Ruby. Ruby gave her a slow nod. "I think it would be good to see those memories. I know how much it comforted Josephine to look at them over the years."

Alice gulped in some air. "Okay. Let's look."

She settled back while Josephine laughed and cried, pointing to the old photos that had kept her daughter alive until her return.

Alice stiffened as she peered at a picture. "I remember," she breathed. "I remember I caught a fish, but I didn't want it to die. I cried and he...dad...my father unhooked it and threw it back."

Eyes full, Josephine grasped her forearm. "Your Daddy was a hard man, but he loved you more than the sun, moon and stars. He called you..."

"Sunshine," Alice whispered, swallowing hard and taking her mother's hand. "Oh, I remember. He called me Sunshine."

She nodded. "Yes."

Josephine reached into her pocket and opened her palm. "It's your locket," she whispered. "Sheriff Pickford let me have it. Your daddy and I picked it out special for you." She paused. "Will you wear it? I understand if you won't want to, right now."

Alice stared at the golden heart. Then she reached out and fastened it around her neck. Tears flowed unchecked down both their faces.

Cooper drew Ruby outside to allow the women some privacy.

Ruby wiped a sleeve across her eyes. "They have so much hurt to get through before they can come to terms with what happened."

"I'm proud of you," he said, wrapping an arm around her shoulders. "You have been a rock for Alice."

"And you've been a rock for me," Ruby said, sending a thrill through him. There was peace in her now, an exquisite comfort that made her even more beautiful. "I was horrible, I said terrible things about Peter."

He turned her to face him. "You were forced into an unwinnable situation, an eagle protecting her nest against someone bent on destroying it. You lashed out."

"Against the guy trying to help save my nest."

He grabbed both her hands. "I'm not holding on to what happened. I wish you wouldn't either." The light teased out the amber depths in her brown eyes as she looked at him and he found himself talking. "I've been thinking," he said, squashing the jitter of nerves in his gut. "That I'm going to stick around for a while. Stay in the cabin to support Peter and help him with expenses."

She kept those luminous eyes on him. "What about your job?"

"I'll commute."

"I'm glad. Maybe we'll see each other more often."

"Would you like that?"

"Yes," she said, gaze flicking away from him. "It's handy to have a botanist around."

"Good, because you still owe me a date."

"I do not."

"Oh, yes. All those years ago, you said you'd go out with me and I intend to collect."

"What if I say no?"

He pulled her close. "You won't."

"So sure of yourself?"

"Yes, I'm sure that I'm a charming guy and I've got serious botanical skills. Wait. Stay right there." His heart thumped a lively jazz tune as he scrambled toward the tall grass and picked a half dozen yellow flowers. She was laughing by the time he returned, swept her a courtly bow and handed her the scraggly bunch. "*Oenothera biennis,* or for the laypeople, the evening primrose. They may not look all that fancy now, but they will open at dusk."

She giggled. "Impressive."

"Ruby Hudson, would you do me the honor of being my girlfriend?"

She blinked. "I thought this was just a date."

"That's just for starters. One date and then a lifetime."

She started, her lips parted in surprise. "A lifetime? You're pretty sure of yourself. What makes you think we'll have a lifetime together?"

"Because," he said, tucking a flower behind her ear, "I love you."

Something warm and sweet pooled in her eyes, a softness that stole across her features and trickled straight into his heart.

"You love me, plant guy?"

"Without a doubt. You're a zany bird-loving, family-loving, passionate nature gal and I could not ask God to design a better partner for me."

She gasped, but he was worried that there was no joyful smile on her face. Had he misstepped? Perhaps he should back off, but there was no chance, no way he wouldn't put it all on the line to have her for his own.

"Cooper, I can't forget what I said." Her forehead creased. "I was happy to see your brother blamed to spare mine."

"And I wondered if your father wasn't covering up to protect Mick, so we're both guilty of loving our brothers. So be it. Guilty as charged." He took her cheeks in his hands, that perfect, freckled face. "I love you, Ruby. I've loved you since I was a kid. Tell me you can love a geeky plant guy who won't eat yellow vegetables and gets his thrills categorizing mushrooms."

She shivered in his arms and then she tilted her head upward to look into his eyes. Slowly, she took one of the bedraggled flowers from her bouquet and stuck one behind his ear to match her own. "You know, I think I can." Then she laughed, a rich, silvery music that filled the forest air.

He kissed her then, long and slow, joy radiating through his body until he thought he might float away into the blue sky.

"But I still think my brother might want to inflict bodily damage on you. He's protective, you know."

"I'm not worried. I'm a good climber and I'm fast. He'll have to catch me first."

She kissed him then, trailing her fingers along his temple and down his neck, sending exhilarating sparks arcing along his spine.

"How did I manage before I had a top-notch plant guy in my life?"

He stroked her hair, wild rejoicing filling his heart. "I have no idea."

Above them, an eagle soared through the forest canopy toward home.

* * * * *

Dear Reader,

Birds are amazing, aren't they? The kings of the sky, they tend to their young and raise families in the face of overwhelming challenges. It seems sometimes that people also face extreme obstacles, scenarios like losing a parent, a spouse and, most horrifying of all, a child. There is no way to protect our nests from the tragedies that come our way. The only peace comes from looking to the Lord and loving each other the best way we can during our uncertain time on this planet. Isn't it an amazing comfort knowing that He loves us, each and every one, from the weakest fledgling to the mightiest eagle?

Thank you for coming along with me on this adventure with Ruby and Cooper. I feel very blessed to have such devoted readers. I am always eager to hear from you. If you'd like to send me a message, you can contact me via my website at www.danamentink.com. There is also a physical address there for those who prefer to correspond by letter.

Fondly,

Dana Mentink

Questions for Discussion

1. Josephine has hope that her daughter will return, even twenty years after her disappearance. What keeps hope alive in the face of overwhelming circumstances?

2. Peter Stokes struggles with alcoholism. How do the effects of that disease change the lives of his family members? How is it possible to thrive in spite of such a family dynamic?

3. What is the best way to hang on to peace in a troubled world?

4. Cooper says accusations can ruin people. Can you recall real-life examples of this happening?

5. How important is it to have a life partner who respects/shares your passions?

6. What is the antidote for broken trust?

7. Have you ever been afraid of learning a truth? What gave you the strength to face your fears?

8. What do you think it means to be a good brother or sister?

9. Ruby asks, "If He makes life, why doesn't He take care of it?" Discuss this.

LARGER-PRINT BOOKS!

GET 2 FREE
LARGER-PRINT NOVELS
PLUS 2 FREE
MYSTERY GIFTS

Love Inspired®

Larger-print novels are now available...

YES! Please send me 2 FREE LARGER-PRINT Love Inspired® novels and my 2 FREE mystery gifts (gifts are worth about $10). After receiving them, if I don't wish to receive any more books, I can return the shipping statement marked "cancel." If I don't cancel, I will receive 6 brand-new novels every month and be billed just $5.24 per book in the U.S. or $5.74 per book in Canada. That's a savings of at least 23% off the cover price. It's quite a bargain! Shipping and handling is just 50¢ per book in the U.S. and 75¢ per book in Canada.* I understand that accepting the 2 free books and gifts places me under no obligation to buy anything. I can always return a shipment and cancel at any time. Even if I never buy another book, the two free books and gifts are mine to keep forever.

122/322 IDN F49Y

Name	(PLEASE PRINT)	

Address		Apt. #

City	State/Prov.	Zip/Postal Code

Signature (if under 18, a parent or guardian must sign)

Mail to the Harlequin® Reader Service:
IN U.S.A.: P.O. Box 1867, Buffalo, NY 14240-1867
IN CANADA: P.O. Box 609, Fort Erie, Ontario L2A 5X3

**Are you a current subscriber to Love Inspired books
and want to receive the larger-print edition?
Call 1-800-873-8635 or visit www.ReaderService.com.**

* Terms and prices subject to change without notice. Prices do not include applicable taxes. Sales tax applicable in N.Y. Canadian residents will be charged applicable taxes. Offer not valid in Quebec. This offer is limited to one order per household. Not valid for current subscribers to Love Inspired Larger-Print books. All orders subject to credit approval. Credit or debit balances in a customer's account(s) may be offset by any other outstanding balance owed by or to the customer. Please allow 4 to 6 weeks for delivery. Offer available while quantities last.

Your Privacy—The Harlequin® Reader Service is committed to protecting your privacy. Our Privacy Policy is available online at www.ReaderService.com or upon request from the Harlequin Reader Service.

We make a portion of our mailing list available to reputable third parties that offer products we believe may interest you. If you prefer that we not exchange your name with third parties, or if you wish to clarify or modify your communication preferences, please visit us at www.ReaderService.com/consumerschoice or write to us at Harlequin Reader Service Preference Service, P.O. Box 9062, Buffalo, NY 14269. Include your complete name and address.

LILPDIR13R